DOG

days

trigger warning
NEW YORK
2025

DOG DAYS is a work of fiction. Any resemblance of characters in this work to people dead, or soon to be dead, is entirely coincidental.

First published as Monastrell Press paperback 001 in March 2012.

Do you understand, gentleman, that all the horror is in just this   that there is no horror!
-A. KUPRIN

Much more affliction than already felt
They cannot well impose, nor I sustain.
-J. MILTON

In the wrong lane
Trying to turn against the flow
I'm the ocean
I'm the giant undertow
-N. YOUNG

DOG
days

intro/ summer 2025

Bicycle riding is my life now. Fixed gear. No brakes. No hands. I move from my *center*, and I move fast. I use my arms too but never on the handlebars. Fixed and *centered*. Your big stupid poisonous *automobiles* do not frighten me. I invented a new style of riding, swimming on land, a sardine king in the shark swarm and if you see it, *when* you see it, you'll know I'm a *singular* sort of man. It looks dangerous. I guess it *is* dangerous, this thing I do. I've decided I'm okay with dying on the bike. But I *lock in*. That's why I'm still alive. Sharks, cops, pit bulls be damned. I am smarter than you. I am faster than you.

I can *bleed*, you understand.
I am not *done yet*.
I am stronger than you.
I *earned* this strength.
So *fuck* you.

***

When I wrote *Dog Days*, my *center* was alcohol. It was my life and it was a glorious fucking life. Alcohol is about death. It is about throwing yourself into the *tide*. I was *tidal*. Now I *am* the tide. I hurt when I remember the women, the cats, the Pennsylvania families of *Dog Days*. It's ancient history, my friends, and I don't think too much of the book. I was fumbling in the dark. In the best moments of *Dog Days*, I am learning about what would be entailed in finally *learning* to write. I was learning to learn. For all its cleverness, its honesty – and it *is* an honest book... I still don't like *Dog Days*. But for me, now, *Dog Days* is a book centered upon what I refer to in *My Kate Like the Seashore* as "the true and accurate rendition."

It is about pain.

It is impossible to know what Sarah, the girl I met in a bar in 2008, really did to me. Or what the violent death of my feline did to me. You don't know about blood. You don't know about meanness. I went to prison for a decade and my cat died, *all* my cats were... murdered, right in front of me, do you understand, they were all *killed*, by lying and idiotic *women*, by *little girls,* and I had no love and no help, I sustained years of violence in prison and now I am old and they sent me to live with raccoons and rats in the tropical forest in a tent under the freeway where I drank 1,000 bottles of good wine, I smoked my cigarettes and missed my dad missed all my days of missing every possible opportunity but I never looked at life as a contest and you silly stupid little people don't know anything about blood which means you don't know anything about life.

Florida is a bacterial *lesson*. I wrote most of *Dog Days* in Michigan and Maryland, living with young women who were predatory and stupid, who were petulant and hopeless and who were whores. I wrote the book in the North but I published it in *Florida*.

That's telling: I went deep into the dirty south to do the *business part*. The *dirty* part. I didn't *want* it to be easy. I don't *respect* easy. No one's ever *treated* me well. I learned my most important lessons while drunk on the beach, unsure of income and in love with my feline soulmate SAM and while publishing 30,000 copies of the simpleminded and aesthetically barren and feline-fixated *Dog Days*.

My cats and I were *morbidly* close. I didn't have *sex* with my cats for two reasons: they were not large enough, and they were *males*. I was in a sense *raised* by cats. I did more than *monitor* these creatures: I invested in them, and I invested heavily. What I was left with is not valid currency in today's society. Maybe not in any society.

I am a *cat man*.

Supremo.

Dog Days is about cats and dogs.

Law of the jungle: might makes right.

But as a poet, as an intellectual, as an *evolved* brute, frequently brutalized by your fellow apes, you find yourself forced to *choose*, between nobility and barbarism.

You choose *poetically*.
You choose a beautiful loser.

You choose a *cat*.

Hopefully, you learn something.

Learn a SECRET.

You live a *secret* life.

Maybe there's a God and maybe He sees this.

Or maybe it's all a lot of canine Nothing. My little book dealt with that much, anyhow. The 2025 world goes out with the tide, as capitalists, always in search of *more*. Their "dealing with nothing" is not at all the same as my own dealing with *Nothing*. Small *n*, big *N*. Fake misanthropes, fake nihilists. Hired romantics. Same imposters, same tourists, same stupid braying and shit-eating dogs, same canine *world* my DOG DAYS was written about.

Only much worse...

I don't let them in anymore....

-Gene Gregorits/ 6.12.25

DOG DAYS

BALTIMORE, MD/
LATE DECEMBER, 2008

It was a straight up rape, after 2 A.M., on Thames Street, with the *Homicide: Life on the Street* building looming in the background. As we approach, we can hear the Mills Brothers' "Someday (You'll Want Me to Want You)" drifting lazily out of an expensive restaurant's shadowy vestibule. The fiend has over- powered his victim and is having his dirty fucking way with her in one of those goofy little Scion cars- not the sedan, but the miniature SUV, which is like a large toaster on wheels. "Only an asshole drives a car like that," my grease-monkey friend Delbert says frequently about many vehicles when we're crossing the blighted plains of suburban Detroit together, and although I am sickened by cars, car prattle, and car worship, I do respect his opinion. But in Baltimore, in this car, submerged in the wet, Lovecraftian murk which rose off the Chesapeake Bay and rolled rogue-like as if smirking at me across the cobblestone streets of Fell's Point, fiend and prey were working it out naturally, developing certain rhythms at times (at 02:15:37 EST her legs encase him, bent at the knees and gripping his hips, her feet curl tightly against the back of his thighs, her hands contort into reptilian things, etching deep, angry grooves into her assailant's clammy shoulders as the passenger side armrest causes the victim mild internal bleeding around her lower back), lapsing into barbarism at others (at 02:31:12 EST there could be heard as far away as the Apex Adult Cinema four blocks north the repeated cracks of her skull against the ridiculous car's windows and dashboard). From a few feet away, had there been any witnesses, the roles assumed within this forced coupling would have been indiscernible, as would their cries, at once more obvious and less ominous than the parked car's strained movements. Had this assault transpired on a weekend, the streets flooded with frat boys and sorority girls and all their attendant vulgarity, it is doubtful that much fuss would have been made of it. But on this calm weekend night, while just a few days before Christmas, belligerent mob activity was nil. The likelihood of such a disturbance alarming the sensibilities of a passerby would seem to be much greater; people cling with a fiery passion to Christian notions of altruism, of brotherly love, sacrifice. But the surreal cognitive shock of inner city violence will set upon the civilized human psyche with the velocity of Category 3 hurricane winds, and sadly, when perilously close to a stranger in crisis, flight is a witness's dominant instinctive reaction. Perhaps, when at a safe distance, the witness will report the incident to local authorities, but the fiend works quickly, the procedural quality and integrity of his transgressions is sacrosanct to him, and unless his mind is torn completely asunder by chemicals or spirits, he will be long gone before any red flashing lights cut through the nightmare's dank old cloth and ectomorphic tendrils, sending the scene crashing back to Earth, from Hell.

I know this to be true, and consider it often, because I am a fiend.

Book One

MURDERLAND STATIONS

-1-

(your precious children)

I'd met with a 24 year old art school dropout called Izabela Slutzky earlier in the day at Lexington Market. There was a heavy, dank air of foreboding, redolent of diesel exhaust, which approached the supernatural in its baleful phosphorescence and which loomed over the already angrier-than-usual Baltimore stink-haze, the cumulative effect being a mournful soak in vaporized bilge water, and cursed with a wretched and eternal hurt, the air thick with ash, so that one was reminded of exactly how far from God one truly was, particularly on this wintry and sullen Baltimore dusk when little Negro children cried but no birds did sing. (Actually, I don't believe there was anything exceptional about the weather at all, but yeah, sure, it was cold I guess, because it was fucking December. And it stank and was damp, sure, because it was fucking Baltimore. But I'm thinking of the pomposity of confused slobs like Izabela, and their monstrous hunger for terrible writing. Jesus wept.)

Izabela studied writing for several years at a prestigious college, because no one had taken the time -or, more likely, no one ever had the good sense to explain to her-that pure writing cannot be taught. She rejected my anti-establishment convictions as the vulgar bigotry of a roughneck menace, a severely troubled autodidact, and similarly failed to see the fundamental wrongness of the gimmick-dependent, Nice Guy Badge-flaunting, publicity-crazed Muppet called Dave Eggers, who she dutifully took on as her own personal lord and savior, along with countless other de-fanged, de-clawed, and de-balled spokesmen for middle class mediocritons and smug little art school cunts. I suppose that chapped my ass a little. (Okay, it chapped my ass a *LOT*. I become something other than sweet-natured when my back is to the wall and

I'm forced into the futile task of trying to explain myself to a silly, simple-minded child with whom I have entangled myself for appallingly shallow and blatantly venal reasons.)

The problem wasn't only Izabela's utterly cosmetic view of and offensively bourgeois approach to the art of writing, but also the deep dissatisfaction I so flagrantly had with my own work. I have to admit, my most recent publications were not going to ensnare the attention nor provoke the affection of any respectable literary agent. First, there was an altogether snide arts and culture book about New York performance artists who commit suicide onstage while engaged in relations (of a sexual nature, obviously) with children, and various farm animals. This book shamed me most deeply, and cost me the love of my parents, which as you'd probably guess, I've always cherished most, above all else. I was the first to announce its obscenity to anyone who'd listen. I also tried to apologize to anyone who cared. But few would listen, and fewer still cared. No matter the remorse I felt, the stigma was indelible and it was eternal: "death for the rotten scum Gregorits and his anti-human, anti-art hatespeak... to hell with him! Don't even mention his name around here!"

Second was a monthly sex diary I wrote for an obscure B-movie journal which had cemented my reputation as a sex pervert and all-round hapless goon, at least in the Maryland/D.C. area where I was currently floundering through a series of farcical trysts exclusively, as it happened, with wealthy young girls enrolled at the legendary Maryland Institute of Cartoon Animals (MICA). These mentally imbalanced, amphetamine-driven sprites demanded of their sex partners prodigious intake of their pharmaceutical speed, which had a profoundly sexual effect on me, debilitating me at times, and best characterized by a crazed obsession with oral copulation, golden showers, and chain smoking. These girls simultaneously and seemingly independent of one another had taken to referring to me as "dirty Gene".

It's true that I was not well, in my writing, in my body, or in my life. It all began in April with the savage murder of my cat, Hank, the world's gentlest little soul, by the pit bulls that completely surrounded my house on Ash Street and who had terrorized all occupants of that house (including a young pug dog, a death metal guitarist, a MICA girl addicted to cocaine, or more specifically, cocaine sex, and a couple of impassioned environmentalists who were also fearsome sociopaths, the kind that make your poor beaten-down Gregorits look like Mary Poppins) for over a year.

I was pleading on my knees one evening before my infernal teenage daughter-fixation, Sarah Tillman. This Lolita-kick of mine had gotten way out of hand: I'd been seeing the globetrotting twenty-something frat- girl since February, and the night of Hank's scourging by redneck terror-dogs, I was in tears, beseeching her to remain with me, making the usual promises, clinging to her-or, rather, the idea of *us*- clinging to this hopeless dream as a drowning man would to a piece of disintegrating driftwood.

The very minute she had given in to my pitiful wailing, there was a commotion outside, and I broke from her embrace to charge down a staircase, over a low wire fence head-on into a gore-smeared pit bull, tearing open most of my fingertips on its teeth in a hopeless attempt to free Hank. His small face was cracked and broken like a beer pretzel. I understood within seconds, in a flash of concentrated lucidity, that my life wasn't worth jack shit anymore, not in Baltimore, or Berlin, or Tokyo, or anywhere, not without Hank... my dearest friend. A fifteen year relationship, all that mattered, was raped and ruined. I understood within seconds that eventually, if I were ever to lessen my grief, the owners of the dogs -and, of course, the dogs themselves- would have to die at my hands.

I slipped into a state of shock.

His death was slow and unimaginably painful. I unraveled quickly and violently, surrounded by degenerate drunks, slobs, and vampires; lost between the crashing waves in my own sea of equal opportunity abuse and neglect.

It was before and during that death-ridden period that I came to love Sarah, the sexiest and most libidinous girl I've known. She had awoken a few good things in me, sparked to life a bit of my old self with her childish invocations and small gestures, who had smothered me, my soul not to keep, with a tender, vulnerable, and trusting gaze such as I had never felt, and the most rapturous of all cunt, who adored me and dreaded me, and it was *too* good in a sense, because the undeniable transience of our affections was always the white elephant in the room, never more omnipresent than during our bleak and prolonged bouts of lovemaking, which continued to escalate in frequency and mutual psychotic determination all the way up to the last one... the all-consuming fear I had of the end could only hasten it, what was a sad, and probably risible affair in the first place; and so it was aborted after I'd become so fatally, unspeakably cuntstruck that I couldn't tie my shoes or count backwards from ten without giving up, my every thought collapsing in a weary, deconstructed heap only moments after arrival.

I groveled, wept, spent weeks crashed out in strange apartments, going through all the slapstick motions of deadly withdrawal. I blubbered and blustered in shifts. That god damned devil Lolita! Seven, ten, a dozen fucks a day! I couldn't get enough of her little body, and all that euphoric, unnaturally good fucking had built up in me like poison. I was a raving jackass, sleeping in creekbeds, moaning like an old ghost in between the blaring of car horns up and down Falls Road. I chain-smoked until my chest rattled and my gums bled. I made it so that in the end, it was easy for her to choose younger, untroubled men, and a new life in New York City, over anything even remotely close to my flaming little death pageant in the dank, unclean Charles Village row home I'd relocated to following the dog violence, my fourth Baltimore residence in less than two years, where I would lay naked and catatonic in the sweltering heat, thinking of the empty Ash Street house 2 miles west, still surrounded by dogs, replaying the audio tapes I made covertly until they disintegrated.

HOME CASSETTE RECORDING, 3431 ASH STREET, BALTIMORE, APRIL 2008.

ST: Did I ever tell you about this friend of mine who would always ask me to fart in his face?
GG: De Sade did that. The Marquis de Sade was always keen

to suck farts, out of prostitutes, right out of their dirty asses, you know. He'd pay them to let him do it.

ST: GENE! That's HORRIBLE! Why would you tell me that?

GG: Because it's true. And you were talking about queefing. And I see how it is, now. Your grade school trash-talk is okay. But when it comes to the serious grown up shit, you turn into a big baby.

ST: Because I can imagine you doing something like that. I bet you have, haven't you?

GG: I was talking about the Marquis de Sade.

ST: You've done ALL the things those freaks do…. All those freaks in your BOOK, Gene!

GG: I don't know what you're referring to.

ST: I don't even want to know. It's not funny! I was gonna let you fuck me again, but now I'm grossed out.

GG: But you were just talking about queefing-

ST: That's a natural physical reaction, to air-

GG: I know what it is, darling girl. My jaw just about hits the floor when you say certain things, because of how you look, I guess.

ST: 15 years old, you mean?

GG: More like 12, actually.

ST: Oh, how nice for you. What things that I say?

GG: Like, "fuck the shit out of me"… *HORRIBLE.*

ST: Hah hah hah! So what? It's NOT horrible. I'm not really a little girl…

GG: Yes you are. Don't ruin it for me.

ST: Just because I *look like* one, hee hee hee.

GG: My little nudie.

ST: No more nudie for you, Humbert Humbert. I'm gonna be…oh GOD! I'm late for *work*! Where are my panties? You *asshole*! You told me you'd kick me out in one hour, and it's been TWO HOURS!

GG: How could I kick you out? I'm crazy in love with you!

ST: But you promised. MOVE!

GG: Oh, you smell good. I've got to lick you a little.

ST: Noooooooo! Don't you see what time it is? STOP!

GG: Oh, you smell *really good.*

ST: I smell like PUSSY! And so do you. MOVE! You're going to go to the bar smelling like that when I leave, to torment

those poor friends of yours. They hate you, you know-
FUCKING.... MOOOOOOOVE! They HATE you, Gene...
they can't stop talking about what an asshole you are the
minute you leave. I've heard them.

GG: I know. And I think you're right, I couldn't smell more
like pussy if I'd... been passed out drunk all night in the, in
the... 50 foot woman's panties.

ST: Who's *the fifty foot-*

GG: No no, it's good to smell like sex. You should know that.
You've lived abroad, right, had orgies, right, in Australia,
where people are heathens like you, and understand that.
You should know all about it. They call it *rooting* down there,
like pigs, *rooting...*

ST: *Please* shut the fuck up. MOVE! I've got to go. Give me a
kiss.

GG: Tonight?

ST: I'll call you.

    -tape cuts-

And with such evocative documents as my soundtrack, I
set immediately to murdering myself, first via starvation,
because I had no money for a pistol, and knew no one who
owned guns. I could not bear the thought of failing yet
another attempt with a blade, so the too-slow starvation
method was followed by an IV overdose of cocaine, which
caused a stroke that did nothing more than leave me
paralyzed for a few days, and then, not without a great
resignation, the blade once again.

I wilted down from 220 pounds to a skeletal 130, and my
most recent razor wounds resulted in an ER visit and
psychiatric evaluation during which I was deemed a threat
and placed under intense supervision. I escaped quickly
when I happened upon an unlocked cabinet containing my
clothes but not my prized motorcycle boots; slipped through
an unlocked door, and over a barbed wire fence early in the
morning, and hotfooted it -shoeless on July Baltimore
asphalt- back to that haunted place where I resumed my diet
of Colt 45, freeloaded marijuana, and one raw egg per day,
usually letting the squalid, clammy afternoons (like NYC,
Baltimore makes its own kind of fecal gravy in the

summertime) pass, minute by miserable minute, with the black folks next door, a pleasant mixture of Vietnam vets, welfare mothers, security guards, and drug dealers.

No one was quite so kind to me during this time, which also included jail, and police beatings, as my neighbors. Pablo was a Special Ops Marine, who'd no doubt killed more men with his bare hands than he could even begin to count. Panda Bear was a lazy bum, whose only interest was in getting high- who could blame him? I can still hear Mama Dolores cackling as I stumbled out onto the porch at 7 A.M. with a warm bottle of malt liquor: "good *morning*, Mister Gene! Oh honey, HOW you doin', baby? I done SAW you crash into that station wagon on your bike yessaday, honey you oughts to be on television!" and then, her customary farewell, "stop to think, and THINK to STOP, awwright baby? You gone be fine, Gene!" 62 years old, in a cloud of pot smoke, loving me more than my own mother, despite my mental illness and my four illegitimate infant children scattered throughout Baltimore City proper. Who knows how many years it would be before I could act as a decent role model to any of them?

I sold my cherished record and book collections to a shop around the corner, caring no longer for anything but booze, sex, and whatever cheap laughter I could find. There was nothing else for me. I had long since stopped going to work. Instead, I took advantage of a gratis video store membership, renting six films a day, shoplifting cheap steaks from the Giant supermarket, and determinedly working up intricate new ploys with which to cheat the righteously stoned young clerks at the Greenmount Avenue Rite Aid out of wine and liquor. I taunted sleazy homicide detectives in the most cutthroat ghetto barrooms and fucked anything in a skirt. I slept behind fried chicken joints with shell shocked veterans, and in the woods behind Johns Hopkins; rescued stray cats from roadsides and alleys in the earlymorning whiskeyfog of bars that opened at 5 A.M., and enjoyed the disgust of those who watched me disappear, a pound, five pounds, ten pounds at a time. This time, I was going all the way, I had the guts for it, finally, and that brought me a strange peace.

It was also at this time that I discovered the legs which

would secure yet another level of damnation, those of the hirsute, gap-toothed Polish dingbat named Izabela Slutsky. This unfortunate surname was pronounced *SLOOT-skee-* "it's SLOOTSKEE, you ASSHOLE," she would protest, but very much in vain because it had for several years been known to all and sundry -except me- that Iz was indeed the most well-fondled, fiddled, faddled, fucked, sucked, shtupped, slippery-dicked, diddled, deep-dished, dorked, dog and ponied, double-derriere'd young dilettante in Baltimore's then-burgeoning Jim Henson and Rocco Zefriedi-influenced "Fraggle Rock Porn" music scene. The frisky little frau fronted an unfunny joke band called "Padre Papoose" that I had always despised intensely, while loitering in doorways when they played the local bars only long enough to visually combine the nastily sexy plumpness of her thighs with the rather off-putting, disingenuously precocious Alfred E. Neumann grin she proudly displayed while stumbling drunk and giggling, loathsomely making a fool of herself through each set of their sloppy indie- rock / cartoon folk garbage. I continued juxtaposing the two images in my fevered imagination to remind me how easily obtainable she seemed, as I power- pumped my pulsating pork in some repugnant men's room, leaving me hormonally crashed so as to be able to enjoy my numbing alcohol sessions without the moronic but hideously potent mania of sexualized grief. It was Izabela whose shows I frequented, because I was becoming in my big fried bean determinedly fixated on those legs of hers, because after only a few months I made the decision that those legs answered something, and I suspect this came about mainly because each of my post-Lolita art school girls was rather tiny and so speed-shriveled that opulent thighs like Izabela's brought me warmly towards something a little more recognizably maternal, a buffer, perhaps, against the unwavering threat of Fatal Panic.

-2-
(talk to my agent)

Izabela was an immigrant, and former prostitute, having grown up in Poland where she apparently learned to be evil personified, already turning tricks at the age of ten in the crude provincial outskirts of Krakow. Her father was a thug ex-mercenary who had helped fill mass graves with women and children during the Balkan wars, and, she liked to remind me frequently, had just been promoted to a rather high ranking position within the Central Intelligence Agency in Langley, VA. Badly worn black and white photos of her old man frolicking at one such death site with Slobodan Milosevich more than quashed any suspicion her claims had aroused.

The night we planned our date was to be my final night in Baltimore. I'd made a firm commitment to myself; the time had come to wash off the wrathful damage of my sins and my sloth, my stinking failure in that hateful city. Sarah, my frat-girl love, was gone, and my tabby, Hank, after having his poor pulverized little body dragged through the court system and disinterred no less than three times (the pit bulls' owner was suing me), was finally rotting alone but in peace, in a barren Jarretsville horse pasture, his grave unmarked save for a $2 plastic rose, a doghouse flower, surely blown into a nearby creek or reservoir by this time. I myself had emerged from a solid 7 months of institutional captivity and gross public scenes, and emerged for just one more, with my only platonic female friend, Kirstie Faust.

I'd been told to remain indoors, as I was by now a marked man, but considerably emboldened by a bottle and a half of my favorite cheap Chilean red (compliments of Rite Aid), we hopped into Kirstie's mangled compact car and drove a mile west to a scummy rock club where I'd had some luck in recent, similar outings. Kirstie was thoroughly disinterested in sex: why bother with such an odious enterprise when the possibility of random psychological manipulation in a crowd of drunkards was perpetually imminent?

She was a striking young creature, with huge scheming eyes, eerily childlike, markedly extraterrestrial in her staggering arrogance and esoteric, delicate mannerisms, and she was always on a Fascism / mind control kick. (She'd taunted me during our first weeks of contact, with amphetamine and nakedness, but I got over it when I realized that the 19 year old scamp was in most if not all ways the intellectually sophisticated and morally bankrupt little sister I'd always wanted but never had.)

Kirstie had enjoyed great success when assisting me in my quests for young women, guiding or re-centering my awkward advances in bars and clubs. She delighted in my swinishness and prurience, basked ecstatically in my willing descriptiveness of the fruits her deeply corrupt sisterly concern would often bear. I was feeling my long-absent beer paunch begin to return, sucking down one Budweiser after another against the bar with the other ruinous and irredeemable bastards. Kirstie elbowed me when Izabela began to approach me from behind. "Quicken up, Gene", she said. At that moment, I felt more than ever before like an older brother to Kirstie. (But an older brother who wants to fuck his little sister.)

Be it the moon, the wine, the culmination of so much doom having such an effect that I was just drained, whatever the cause, I was relaxed and confident that night. Any shyness exhibited was false, and Izabela and I chatted for over an hour, mostly about her last lover's foot-long penis. She called the young Lothario a "chew toy" (which effectively destroyed her youthfulness, immediately causing me to think of her as not only a dirty whore, but an OLD whore), confiding also that a 12 inch dick is just the most wonderful thing, because "you feel like you're still being fucked the next day." I nodded politely, hoping that she was drunk, and not *really* a disgusting pig of a whore. He of the freak-penis was acting manager at the arthouse cinema where, arguably, I was still employed (the nature of this confusion was such that the subject of my employment was consciously avoided by the managers... after all, it brought with it a feeling of arcane knowledge of the unspeakable, of malevolence, coming out of some darkness of evil, and my true status there was and would remain forever shrouded in mystery. No one, not me, not even the theater's owner could remember if I'd been fired, and the entire staff- save for the underage workers, whom I plied with booze and dope- was afraid to approach me in my skeletal condition, or to even look in my direction as I walked through the lobby, muttering curses to myself and openly slurping down pints of Evan Williams or Old Grand Dad... so I came and went freely, collecting no paycheck, but coffee and chocolate bars aplenty, staying abreast of film culture, sometimes sleeping in the back rows of one of the five auditoriums for 3 or more consecutive nights, such as when the best film of 2008, *In Bruges* returned for a weeklong run).

I informed Izabela of my permanent departure from Baltimore in the next week, and apologized that there wasn't time to get to know each other a little better. We were interrupted every four seconds by yet another young hipster fellow, his many delicate manufactured affectations invariably rising from him as infection seeps from a suppurating wound. Conversation transpired nonetheless. I don't remember anything she said (anything unrelated to my employer's genitals, that is), as even then, despite the fact that neither of us could or would admit it, the attraction was, though mutual, a purely physical thing. She too, in her swaggering infantilism, in her "fuck me" skirt and "fuck me *harder*" calfskin boots, saw me as a Dirty Loser, and I, in my compromised/ contaminated idealism, in my basement-scented hobo rags, saw her as a ditzy piece of art-school tail worth the abusive array of Cat Power or Bright Eyes albums she'd inevitably force me to listen to in her car.

That night, I reminded myself what outsized egos rock'n'roll singers, even lousy ones, nurture and cultivate daily, and how this is permissible and even encouraged in female singers particularly... and stripped of romantic pretense, I allowed myself to push for a good old fashioned one night stand, on *that* night. Perhaps if I'd been quicker to determine how little she understood or appreciated the very things she claimed to love most urgently, chiefly writing, if I'd known what a homicidal, hate-fueled cunt this cougar-in-training truly was.... but in a lifetime of regrets, Izabela was only one more.

There was to be no late night meeting, romantic pretense or otherwise. Instead, I agreed to an afternoon lunch date, less than 72 hours before my final departure from this city, to which I had vowed never to return. The morning before this date (I suggested the Lexington Market, for its considerable romantic potential), I staggered from an all night drinking session at a frat house littered with middle aged eccentrics spouting "hipster" rubbish, where I felt the doom once again, from out of nowhere, and so slashed my wrists with a brand new Wilkinson Arms double edged razor blade I had found in my coat during the 5 block walk home.

-3-

(all things put together)

Our first date commenced then at the Lexington Market, an oceanic wallop of fecundity, a swirling carnival of base pleasures which does merit a thorough rendering. Imagine the choking olfactory bluster of stale sweat, raw meat, cooking meat, disinfectant, fish funk, deep-fry grease pits, and fresh baked goods that any large and ancient inner-city market lays singular claim to, and top that off with cheap whiskey, cigarette smoke, human shit, and more fish funk. Imagine a massive indoor sprawl of over 500 vendors, tables, stalls, booths and counters encompassing the cuisine of every significantly industrialized nation on earth, except for, perhaps, France, and imagine that stifling odor met or exceeded by the number and concentration of human bodies (either drunken and useless, or speed-cranked and grossly overdrawn) creating the vaguely sub-Roman spectacle person by person, each with his or her own special role, in all their various un-magical endeavors, carried out until death arrives, and then you have it: a sensory immersion which maybe itself is somewhat magical, and certainly outdoes any urban market experience *I've* ever had. Also, you're never more than 50 paces from a large, well-stocked liquor stall, and you're the only white person there. Wonderful.

I'd had the routine down, having haunted the Lex regularly since making the most catastrophic choice of my life three years earlier, when I fled Detroit for Baltimore. The routine developed quickly, first hitting the Korean-operated pizzeria for their daily special of $2.50 Heinekens (from the bottle, but served in a white plastic cup), then savoring the crowd, the hawkers and spooners, the choplickers and hammerheads, the strawberry tarts and stingray pimps, the phebes and the phoids, the dinks and the coffee addicts, but best of all, the odd corpse, freshly expired: what fantastic joy in discovering one before the janitors! And never a cross word spoken, never an angry voice, drunkards retiring quietly to hide in the Satanic stench of the restrooms until recharged, ready to rejoice righteously in the rarified market air. I'd spend $2 at the Japanese stall, $3 at the Korean stall, another 4 on authentic Mexican tacos, maybe throw a few to one of the thirteen seafood merchants, keeping the beer flowing, a good, hearty *nosh* there in the roiling morass of SERIOUS HUMANITY.

I'd been waiting for only a minute or two, standing at one of the tables in the west end's lower level dining platform, when Izabela arrived, wearing black leggings and a tight elastic skirt. Her hair was a mess. The vibe was BAD. I gave her a quick, impersonal hug, distrustful of her intentions, and took her first to the beer stand, then to the adjacent sushi counter. We adjourned to the dirty dining area on the second level, where she questioned my heavily bandaged arms, and asked me if the rumors about me being a heroin addict were true. I told her the wounds were moving accidents, and she narrowed her crusty eyes dramatically. I explained as delicately as I knew how that anyone who told her that I was a junkie was obviously trying to scare her away from me because I was a sex fiend, a wolfen rapist, and a putrid alcoholic. This "bad boy" routine works so well it's sickening. But little did I know then how supremely revolted her friends were by the lumbering specter of me: "Crazy Gene", "Scumbag Gene" or, as her winsome art school playmates seemed to insist upon, "old writer dude". Of course, most of them had carnal knowledge of this girl, but I was confident, being an old crazy scumbag writer dude, that I could steal the closest thing these soft young boys had to a diva. I hadn't lifted a finger, hadn't stuck out my little toe that night, but, apathetic and careworn in my mid-thirties, had simply leaned there grunting and sucking suds, letting her do all the work and embarrass herself, learning the pros and cons of a freakishly large unit from a morbidly passionate size queen. That's what works best for me, you see: as long as I can keep my big stupid mouth shut...

And she continued: "I saw you one night on 36th Street. You were smoking in front of Townie's Bar, and I said to my friends, 'now *that's* the guy I want.' Don't blush!"

"I'm not blushing."

"You *are* blushing. Anyway, I thought you looked like James Dean, standing there," she said with a broad, boastful sweep of her right hand.

I gave her the asshole grin, I couldn't help it. I was working on a beer buzz, and that got me thinking, *keep going, honey. Maybe Heath Ledger, as well? A bit of Frankenstein's Monster?*

"My friends all know you. They said, 'that's Gene, he's a junkie'."

I drained my cup and said, "well, a drug addict isn't necessarily a junkie. I believe they may have their terms confused."

"And they said you were an alcoholic. They said you'll Fuck anything in a skirt."

"What makes them so high and mighty? From what I've heard, those M.I.C.A. kids are fucking scumbags."

"Uh huh."

"Yeah, they do all the same shit I do. It just doesn't seem as bad, because they're all Muppets. If you talk and act and dress like a fucking retard, you can get away with anything."

"Uh huh. That's brilliant, Gene."

"Well anyway, I don't use heroin. That's a nasty lie."

A sarcastic art school girl was looking at me over a greasy table like I was a test monkey and I didn't want to care. I'd already been fed to the pit bulls by one insatiable heathen who gleefully danced on my grave. I was reduced to the level of a mange-ridden half- Mongol creature who hangs out behind the Kroger supermarket, caked in his own feces from licking his own asshole, rising only once a day to tell jokes for quarters until security guards half-heartedly chase him into hiding. It was only a matter of time, maybe a month, maybe a year, before I snapped and embarked on a string of hyper-violent knife murders, painstakingly researched to insure that Total Damage was inflicted upon those (including myself) whom I held responsible.

Warming up on beer, we talked, mostly about my nasty

reputation. I was becoming fed up with the subject: she was annoying. But I'd made the trip already, all the way from Charles Village, so I remained, and serviced her ego without shame when I confessed to what I chose to call "infatuation" (although I didn't specify which part of her specifically I was infatuated with).

Izabela confessed to being drunk already, so after trespassing throughout the Lex's many narrow maintenance and management corridors, running at a good clip, pretending to be lost, behaving offensively, like a pair of those suburban middle-class Noxema babies in a piece of shit John Hughes movie (but Izabela found those movies endlessly charming). After insincerely proposing that we collaborate on an article about the place (interviewing the janitors and such), we began to make our exit, eliciting hostile stares from the crowd on our way. I kept an arm around her waist, navigating our way through a particularly hairy throng of juiceheads and panhandlers, as if afraid for her safety or concerned that she was too precious to remain among the rabble one second more than necessary. Of course, it is those very people who have my deepest respect, and in a sense, we'd been trespassers the minute we entered the market, because Izabela advertised herself as a kind of aristocratic airhead, rather than a guest in someone's home.

This sort of deliberate straying into a house of "other" is normally something I'll permit myself when alone, because the natural guilt and self-consciousness I feel is, if not fleeting, then at least minimal, and held in check by whatever level of derangement, estrangement, or basic meanness I'm experiencing that day (and also, by the guilt of others, which you can see quite plainly on so many smash--nosed faces).

Those feelings run deep, stubbornly, and they are such that my presence is not challenged, maybe not even resented. My scars must count for something here. But with an exhibitionist skank on my arm, I am not the same feral creep, now softened, perhaps celebratory in my mood, a normal no-good oh-fay motherfucker... I then appear in the eyes of the hardcore Lex regulars as a sore thumb, an insensitive gloater, a contemptuous little shit, a grinning punk *way* out of his depth, dependant upon police for his safety, a tourist, a rubbernecker, all manner of things no one but those actual smug cocksuckers would ever want to be associated with, much less mistaken for.

But it's true, the Lex summons forth some comforting voices in me. I can drink there and melt into it all with ease, the hours skulking by like bored alley cats, in the blur of wide open, public sensory distortion, in a rare, uncorrupted place that allows for thought, allows BREATH to enter my lungs, and I'm readied for some meaningful, thoughtful, soulful exchanges with my fellow man. Yet I am exceedingly picky when it comes to companionship there.

Several months before, my first date with Sarah transpired at the Lex, and on that day I did not drink at all, instead focusing all of my available energy on making the most of what I suspected was a clear head and a bright mood. I limited myself to casual observations, and never let my enthusiasms or my staccato narration grow tiresome or strident, holding it *together*. I did not mumble, as I often do out of nerves, I did not babble or lisp or soapbox. On that day, I was COOL, my last twenty bucks, no cigarettes, and "anything you want, baby, I'm *loaded*!" On that day, I was sober as a hanging judge and concerned only with her happiness. I played "normal" as we toured the market from one end to another, then back again, without any discomfort or worry or fear. We were smooth and sober and attentive to each other, we were in love and letting a beautiful day just happen, as one so seldom does. I found a way to lose myself a little in those crowds with her as I did alone, and the old men smiled at us as we walked past. There was in Sarah and I both a profound respect for their tolerance of us, for their endurance, a gratitude for their acceptance, an acute awareness that their old school toughness, all that mean street cool, made our short time there something more than it would have been without them, somewhere else with a middle class crowd for example, such as the collegiate hordes of Federal Hill. Like me, I believe Sarah's experience there was permeated by an implicit awareness that anything we lacked, or that any aspect of us in which we, for any multitude of possible reasons, were somehow lacking, was nonetheless an essential component of *this*, and was therefore unassailable, utterly without fault, because *this* was perfect: our romance writ large on their walls and in their time. And I was maybe a bit sheepish, but it was light we brought with us that day, it was a glow I gave off because of her, and those poor old bastards saw it. A few even winked at me, perhaps sensing that she was too good for me.

Leaving the Market, this 5"2' Irish/Italian beauty looking all the world like Olivia Hussey in the 1960s, with her brown hair and after-storm eyes, pulled herself up to me and kissed my cheek: "thank you for the most perfect date ever". I am left with a kind of delirium, of both detachment and an aggressive, almost bludgeoning wonderment when reflecting on it today, astounded by the notion that something as superficially unremarkable as a Lexington Market date can assume such proportions, and even more shocking that the day was exceptional in the minds of us both, in the same moment, on the same spot, without even a week of alcohol abuse to begin the dimming of the sharp neon, the obscuring of the rough edges, the muting of traffic sounds, through memory loss, the process by which the mundane becomes mythical. We shared this in real time, and a homeless man's eyes screamed at me across the market, as I stood board- stiff and disoriented a few feet from the ladies' room door, they seemed to say: "are you finally happy?"

Walking there on my first date with Izabela, a mean spirited and vulgar child who possessed none of Sarah's sweetness, I did feel as I feared I might on that day with Sarah. She was gone and what was left could not sustain me, so I simply let the beer work its effect, losing myself falsely in the possibilities of the hours ahead, in which Izabela would either remain at my side, or not. I suppose I was jubilant when she agreed to accompany me further into the evening, but not in a reverential way of being jubilant, as you might be without skepticism or unease, inhabiting your truest and purest self, as it were... but rather like a ferocious crack rush, or soaking up the 3rd rate glory of pulling off some petty thieving bullshit, of scoring drugs or cheating on your spouse or kiting a bad check, when you know your luck is shot but getting away with it one more time, OUT of time, feels good for all the wrong reasons. And while I did implicitly understand that Izabela, even more than Sarah, intended only to use me for some cheap danger, the arrangement was fine by me as long as I could get her out of those black leggings and spread her chubby thighs wide open.

We snaked our way through Fell's Point, bar hopping, flirting ferociously, settling finally on a small punk rock dive a block from the water, where I'd found myself one dark night shortly after I'd moved to Baltimore, hopelessly lost in the strange cobblestone streets after midnight. I explained to her the sinister nature of having my two year Baltimore residence bookended by nighttime drinking sessions, both entirely by chance, in the same little Fell's Point dive. We spoke openly about our past promiscuity, our families, books we liked. She seemed to find me sincere, if disturbed, and I was wondering if I'd misjudged the girl, for the talk came easy, and I wasn't faking my laughter.

The night was going better than most, my composure holding out unnaturally long, because without the stimulant of nicotine (I was not smoking), panic did not attack my entire nervous system as angrily. Still, I was rosy-hued and a guzzling fool, encouraging Izabela to down shots of liquor with me, even sneaking extras from the barmaid, our new friend, while my date was in the ladies room. As would become our tradition during the ensuing three month affair, Izabela and I necked without guile or tact all the way down Thames Street, back to her obnoxious vehicle.

-4-

(kangaroo courting)

AFTERNOON: radio static and spiders and silverfish abound in a cozily furnished but unfinished cellar storage room. A newly acquired rescue beast, claws the size of tennis balls, all hissing fleabitten bobcat hatred: SAM. He was the neighborhood stray until the neighborhood stopped feeding him. I was his choice, and what choice did he leave me? And a cheap shag carpet, bookshelves with bottles, no books, the DVD menu for Martin Scorsese's *Gangs of New York* repeating endlessly on the 27 inch Philips monitor, high volume alcohol soreness, jackhammer in my head... sexy little Kirstie's Chuck Taylor sneakers at my transom window, her god damned Camel Light carbon monoxide causing surges of self-righteous loathing and contempt for the vile habit. Shady old Barclay Street is jumping, Northwest Baltimore only inches from my heavy clouds of dreamstuff and bladder-denial, my feet cold, my dick hard.

At night my lair was like a street theatre, the naked bulb flooding the Barclay asphalt with light when the sun goes down, and Bryan Ferry songs, a beacon, an invitation, warm and private, you might like to come inside, snuggle up, get a glass, but it is no longer night, and I'm smiling into my gore-caked pillow, remembering bits of Izabela and Thames Street, then remembering *all* of Izabela and Thames Street, no longer smiling: RAPE! Surely, the police would be on my doorstep before I could find my bathrobe or make some tea. Not even a vitamin drink or a shower. I couldn't move, because This is what Happens. Isn't it? When you drink? Strap yourself in, and say you're sorry. I could only wait, the horror no longer even new, but ugly as ever.

Over the radio and the annoying U2 song from *Gangs* came the sound of air being blown into still water, vigorous bubbling, a "ringtone", the announcement of an incoming call picked up by jerry-rigged pirate Internet hardware, so I swept the covers off myself and the bobcat, made a dive for the desk, the computer, the keyboard, fumbled for the cheap Radio Shack microphone, clicked the "accept" button with the mouse.

SKYPE CONVERSATION– PAMELA© CALL RECORDER TRANSCRIPT 12.21.08 (13.52.16 EST)

Caller: Gene?

GG: Yeah.

Caller: It's Izabela.

GG:

Caller: Good morning? Hello?

GG: Look, I'm really sorry, I know I got a little-

Caller: Rough?

GG: How are you?

Caller: BRUTAL! God, you were SO rough.

GG: Yeah. How-

Caller: You are insane. You're just an insane person.

GG:

Caller: What are you doing right now?

GG:

Caller: I'm gonna hang up.

GG: You wanna come over? I'll make you breakfast.

Caller: Yeah, yeah. Half hour?

GG: Sure.

Caller: Okay.

After a scalding hot shower and a close shave, I was raw from a not-yet-beaten hangover, ringy and hyper. I began cleaning the house fitfully, emptied of everything except black tea and hormonal fireworks. The Scion pulled to the curb while I wiped down the table and counters of the house's communal kitchen. I was beating some eggs with a fork when a most pleasing shape appeared through the curtained windows of the front door and the violent doorbell made me spasm and whimper, speed-pulsed with a heart murmur and a hard-on. I turned down the right wing talk radio I listened to for cheap laughs and let Izabela in.

We spent the next several days together, mostly in my

bunker-like cellar bedroom. I took full advantage of the opportunity to smother her with attention, engaging in many of the things I'd loved doing with Sarah: cooking, drinking wine, watching films, and screwing. Izabela and I cavorted like pigs at least four times in the evening, and always at least once in the morning. I gave her the good news in alleyways, storage areas, public restrooms, movie theatres, parking lots, and small wooded areas all over Baltimore. I sleepwalked through the public and social rituals. I uttered every term of endearment on auto-pilot, not knowing or caring whether it was simply post-traumatic stress disorder which distanced me, or Sarah, or a very real and increasingly acute dislike of Izabela. It was hard to tell, because I'd taken a considerable step out of my own reality, and had come to accept all things as by remote. I observed the various occurrences and random events from afar, with an objective curiosity that only flagged at night; I re-inhabited my subjective mind fully when inebriated, which also made me a shameless pussy freak. We were tender with one another, mostly, yet through her girlish adoration I sensed skepticism, related most directly, I presume, to my poverty and alcoholism. While insufferably impudent, Izabela was now in love with me.

News of this rippled throughout her art school community, causing something of a scandal. She thrived on the discomfort of others; that had been obvious to me from the beginning. We couldn't walk ten feet in public without bumping into a student from the Maryland Institute of Cartoon Animals. She delighted in introducing me to one manufactured ragamuffin after another. The Muppets were unanimously disturbed by her razor ravaged new "chew toy", concerned to the point of visible worry for their vulnerable and witless young Izabela. She'd made the less-than-judicious choice of beaus a longstanding tradition. Now, nothing could touch the unrestrained grandeur and prestige of the role I knew I'd bumbled into: Satan. An unearthly demon spirit feasting on the souls of innocents, ruthless and primal, I was the sum of Charles Manson and his Topanga Canyon Freaks,the reincarnation of that fat pig charlatan Aleister Crowley without the retarded Luciferian shock-jive. And I had DIPLOMATIC IMMUNITY. An entire community of slovenly slackers forced by the stranglehold of their own suffocating scene-vamp manners and hippie affectations to swallow every swollen insult which begged for release, forced to eat their own outrage as I too went through the motions of dishonest civility, shaking hands and laughing pleasantly, privately aghast at the unchecked narcissism and infantilism on display before me. I was no longer sleepwalking, but quivering in mortal shame, for I had been shoved roughly before THE ENEMY: urban bohemia. It was a world I'd always lingered tentatively on the outskirts of, not belonging to the roughneck legions either, but caught rather inexorably in a spectral no-zone between mutually exclusive parties, both of which were teeming with the fevered bloodlust and unrelenting sadism of a million treacherous, piss-brained cunts.

Izabela's albino roommate, Wendy Querelle Rothstein-Worthington, was a frumpy, overbearing megalomaniac who looked like an exceptionally ill- humored lesbian. She had a bulging frontal lobe, beady little black eyes, and like Izabela, was always sorely in need of a bath. But Wendy Querelle Rothstein- Worthington was *not* a homosexual. In fact, she was an insatiable groupie who routinely left her heartbroken main squeeze (a sweet-natured, Fozzie Bear-ish gent named Thurston) to hungrily service the American Eurotrash icon Vincent Gallo. The painfully aloof young Wendy Querelle Rothstein-Worthington would squirm and flail and fidget upon the cluttered front room's red velvet sofa like a hypersexual 7 year old, feigning rage, ennui, restlessness, and fatigue as the mood struck her.

I was warned by Izabela, who worshipped the bristling femi-Nazism of Wendy Querelle Rothstein-Worthington, to stay on her good side, and to never make eye contact with her. I was also forbidden from drinking in the home. Wendy Querelle Rothstein-Worthington, a New Age priestess who worked as a hair stylist in an "organic hair salon", had announced the arrival of her "professionalism" at age 24 with a swearing off of drugs and alcohol, and all those "welcome within the Rothstein-Worthington sanctum" were honored with the highest trust: a gesture of respect for her chastity, by making the Rothstein-Worthington vow oneself, was automatically assumed of all guests.

I thought Wendy Querelle Rothstein-Worthington was a hellish nightmare of a human being, and said as much to Izabela, furiously warning her that Western civilization, or indeed the entire planet, could drift as deeply into the vagina-rule of the modern age as they-or the cosmos (or the femi- Nazi cunt) demanded, while I could not possibly EVER submit to such debasement for something as tawdry and ridiculous as fucking), reminding her that by comparison to the soul rape of allowing oneself to be pussy-whipped by a bohemian grotesque such as Wendy Querelle Rothstein-Worthington, drag queens -or "chicks with dicks"- seemed a healthy and reasonable alternative. I also explained that, bearing in mind the inhuman misery poor Thurston had adapted to during his indentured servitude with the cunt, it seemed only decent and compassionate that I go to him immediately and beat him into the nearest emergency room with a hammer, iron bar, or similar object which, if used correctly, might relieve him of his identity and, one would hope, his shame.

Izabela laughed, but I no longer remember how she defended her mentor on that occasion, or *if* she defended her at all: I had already begun to tune her out automatically, because she was never anything less than petulant and disrespectful. I focused instead on the logistic practicalities of my upcoming move out of Baltimore. I was returning to the city of my birth, Harrisburg, where my bastarding bureaucrat brother Mike had secured a cheap efficiency apartment from a colleague of his, a bloated hog and slimeball yuppie son of a bitch who owned property in the same gay neighborhood I'd lived in back in 1995, when I worked the graveyard shift at the YMCA, acting as a quasi- chicken pimp and petty extortionist.

After resuming a 15 year old security guard position for the Pinkerton Agency, I was to remain in Harrisburg for a minimum of six months: enough time to glue my head back together, finish my novel, re-pay the grand I owed my father, and put away enough dough for another move south, this time to Savannah, GA, where I would do nothing but rent a clapboard shack, and work dog labor. I would lay on the beach with the other clapboard shack dwelling dog laborers and be, just *be*.

I lay semi-prostrate upon Izabela's dirt-strewn bed, thinking about Harrisburg, dreading the town yet almost delirious with excitement at the prospect of leaving Baltimore. Izabela lived in Wendy's basement,a vastly different type of bunker than my own, which was by comparison a rustic vacation cabin on the Northern California coastline. Izabela's bunker was an eye-wrecking institutional white from floor to ceiling. Barren and freezing cold, even in the summertime she told me, the uninviting sterility was offset by the presence of a poorly maintained litter box and waist- high mounds of unwashed clothing, amid which jutted belts, shoes, CDs, photographs, notebooks, and multi- colored bottles of hair product. Izabela's loathsome lavatorial lair somehow managed to be at once German sophisticate art-slob and acne-ravaged Kentuckian meth-head. Several cheap Ikea bookshelves crammed tight with an impressive array of titles confirmed that, while our taste in writers was far from similar, we could at least push new material on each other.

This was heartening to me; Sarah was a frat girl whose pussy got wet when she thought of the fight to end world hunger; she read books by Mitch fucking Albom. Leslie before her had read only one book in her lifetime: Motley Crue Unauthorized. My own library was almost completely wiped out for the summer's rent and drinking money. Izabela loaned me a stack of books by Pynchon, Rimbaud, Grass, Capote, and others. I wondered how a woman so well-read could be so airheaded, refusing to dismiss her vapidity as a symptom of her tender age. *I* wasn't like that at 24,was I? In any case, she snapped at me when I selected a lurid 60s pulp novel called *I Spit On Your Graves*, rebuking me for my rotten taste.

"It figures you'd gravitate right to the trashiest piece of shit book I've ever bought."

I beamed with demented pride, and became vaguely fond of Izabela in that fleeting moment. We dropped down onto her unclean sheets, she whining and grunting like a harpooned seal pup, while I tried to pretend she was Ellen

Barkin. It was a rotten trap I'd found myself in. I was a somnambulant casualty, tormented beyond hope, and far past the point of disentangling myself.

Before we were finished, Izabela asked me if I wanted her to speak Polish. Guys always liked the immigrant bit.

"Oh. No... no, that's alright," I said.

Immediately afterwards, I flooded her womb with my acrid booze-cum. I slept soundly for a few hours in the never-washed bedsheets, drooling absently into the cum stains of other young men, other afternoons and other evenings, while upstairs, Wendy Querelle Rothstein-Worthington made a vegan feast for pallid, anemic Christmas revelers and danced unemotionally to a ZZ Top record.

When I woke, Izabela was gone. I got out of bed and plucked three pieces of fresh cat shit off the floor with a fabric softener sheet.

I shivered. I gagged.

Would I ever find a civilized town? Was there a kind woman somewhere?

And was it snowing like this tonight in Jarretsville, over that field where I laid down my old friend? I guess that's where I really was. I knew my life had to be over. If there was a chance, I didn't want it.

But "keep fighting", that's what I was told. In the meantime, all I had was fucking Izabela. Fucking Baltimore. Fucking booze. I slumped up the stairs, through the party, and into the snow outside. There was nothing in that night but alcohol, in places where I was not exactly popular. Well, one more night couldn't hurt, could it? I lit a cigarette and started north towards 36th street, crunching slowly and clumsily through small snowdrifts, block after block of ugly, cheaply built old row homes, kicking in the occasional car door, wincing at the taste of my bloody gums and the sight of it all.

-5-

(pole cat + pit kill)

I was with Pablo, ex-Special Ops, USMC, at Kitty's on Greenmount Avenue. Kitty's was like a hug and a kiss from your mother, if your mother is the state penitentiary. Kitty's was the snakepit: blood stains. Kitty's was the shithole: Packaged goods. Kitty's was cops and ex-convicts all in a row, murmuring in the afternoon about Central Booking, or guns, or knives, or new drug enforcement policies, or dead people. Kitty's was the same cops and cons at night, screaming about card games, or dope hustles, or women.

At 6'8" and 260 pounds, Pablo surely felt cramped in there. Kitty's, on an average evening, could appear almost impenetrable. It was a bar which required strange variations on the typical hairpin turn or tiptoe slide, between a regular patron and the takeout cooler, with new patrons arriving and blocking the checkout counter as you're navigating your way though the crowd of poor blacks and the occasional weirdo white, always a cop. Pablo drank Budweiser and barked didactic Marine corps rebop, at tiresome lengths that would temporarily dissolve any personal fondness because he was in those moments a boorish blowhard drunk, a large one you didn't dare interrupt or contradict and certainly never hush. In Pablo's conversational death grip, one understood that this man did not concern himself with your comfort or lack thereof. One suspected that the more visible to him your twitches and squirms, the greater his determination to impress and to educate. I'd never understand the Marine corps experience. His passion was as close as I'd ever come, and I wanted to be close, but as he shifted his weight from one leg to another, clarifying one acronym or slang term after another, and all those Marine thug platitudes, my predominant ills drifted from me, along with my vagrant "freedom", in all its fictitiousness. I'd lost my own war; Pablo shared his by force.

Pablo: "why you be killin the man's dog? What the Fuck he do to you? That's some evil shit, brother."

"I told you. This little scar-faced hippie cunt, it was her dog did the actual killing. There's *three* dogs, altogether. The man, he's the other neighbor, alright? His dogs tore around the place unchained for months before this happened. His girlfriend, she's a lawyer, this lawyer bitch cunt came to the aid of the hippie cunt in court, after she'd made claims that my animal was rabid, which meant I had to provide a tissue sample, which meant I had to go back out to this fucking field where I didn't want to leave him in the first place and I had to dig him up with a fucking pick axe- wait, man... it's a long story. But I can't have any fucking dignity in this fucking life until those fucking dogs are fucking dead do ya get that?"

"I'm with ya; it's about respect, alright? I feel that. So, it's two dogs."

"There's three of them, altogether. I wouldn't kill dogs or anything else if I didn't have to-"

"Yeah, I know you ain't like that. But still... you be seein' me out front there in the morning with that old hound? That my Froggy, and we go back a way. Up on ten years, must be. And I don't see the love lost over no nasty cat, how you be sayin, but you say he important to you, and I can get with that. And you gettin punked here, look like, so... I'll tell ya....best way... you gotta kill a dog...best way be anti-freeze...that show up in the blood as Parvo."

"What's Parvo?"

"Dog disease. Some kinda worm cause it. Parvo."

"Well, I ain't too worried about covering my tracks. They're ignorant, these fuckers, but they ain't stupid. I just want the shit to work."

"Anti-freeze, Gene. Put it in...put it in some...beef chuck, burger meat, whatever. S'all it is. Real simple. Okay? Show up in the blood as Parvo."

"Anti-freeze. That's cheap."

"Yeah, 's right. At's'm *nasty cold* shit. Fuckin snake's what you bein. Don't come cryin when you kill them dogs and you feelin shameful. And man's gotta come back on ya, you kill his dog. "

I left Pablo there at the bar, and made my way across Greenmount to buy a case of Miller High Life, and a jug of anti-freeze.

Back at home, I found a crudely scrawled note:

"GENE, YOU ARE OUT JAN 1.NO DISCUSION" (sic). I took my beer downstairs, and the anti-freeze, sat down on the bed with Sam and thought about the dogs. I thought about Harrisburg and the moving arrangements. My brother, the rugby champion, had secured an apartment for me. My father was footing the first, last, and security deposit. My favorite bartender was offering to drive the truck for me. And then there was Izabela. As all of normal society encroached then upon Christmas, in those final days of 2008, I continued hung and hooked like wet laundry, in my effortless drift toward Izabela, or rather hanging there in my slothful gazing out at this drift as it occurred, morbidly diverted, half-narcotized, trapped in this gaze which was perhaps not so unbreakable or even effortless, but with some premeditation, a passively cruel inaction on my part, opportunistic, at the very worst predatory.

But as I say, I was not, *could not be*, entirely certain of my motives or of the nature of my decision making, or of my own heart, as Izabela enjoyed doing all of the work: showing me around in the bars, buying and preparing meals, openly demanding to be wantonly sodomized. I left welts and bruises upon her chubby frame from neck to ankle, unable to consider it rape. Anything short of striking Izabela directly with a closed fist seemed to excite her sexually. She reveled in the public flaunting of our cartoonish affair; I would find myself in her car pondering it all, and as winter light sparkled through her semi-afro (a frazzled and befouled garden of auburn Eastern European hair, like so much chaparral), so too would shine inside me the notion of the two of us, as a legitimate and respectable young couple (if necessarily outside of Baltimore, where her jealous ex-suitors and my illegitimate offspring were omnipresent). I would insist upon the inherent superficial benefits of constant physical attention from a frisky young girl provided that I could assume of myself a certain responsible distance, and never come to seek or desire the worshipful kind of love (for me, the only love acceptable as "pure") which she could not genuinely inspire nor I (as my recent past so gruesomely demonstrated) support. If so enabled and so inclined, with a compromised love by no means beautiful, but not unpleasant, maybe I could return to the business of writing, and of existing in the world as a complete being, moving about with purpose and awareness, making a last-ditch bid on health and on humanity.

Izabela busied herself with school, where she attended "poetry workshops" and took a psychology class. For some time, she'd been employed as a social worker, assisting autistic, retarded, or otherwise disadvantaged persons with the carrying out of their daily chores. She would call me on her cellphone during these excursions, from a shopping center, or grocery store. Her "individual" (this was the only acceptable term for them) would sometimes be audible in the background, gibbering excitedly: a disruptive shriek of some unknowable ecstasy would explode from the lungs of the subnormal man, thus interrupting Izabela's own mundane sing-song narrative or strenuously affectionate interrogation of my own day's events (which I would always fabricate, very much in vain).

Her individual's helpless unleashing of mucous-rich flailing and lashing about in retail stores did not embarrass Izabela in the slightest. Quite the contrary, she would become euphoric, barely able to contain her joy at the man's involuntary self-immolation. Her voice on the phone was an unwaveringly petulant and self- conscious expression of a supreme self-fulfillment; which was in fact a lie, generated and driven by an inestimable and all-too-palpable viciousness, which a discerning and reasonably cognizant lover could experience only as something potentially Satanic. Izabela's voice had a quality of insidious insincerity, and when she called me during an errand with an individual (each of whom she'd bestowed with an overtly disparaging moniker: "farter", "diaper freak", "boon boy", and so on), the juxtaposition of her unnaturally exuberant social performance with the individual's primal high notes would stir in me a vague fascination, as a writer (for material), as a student of human folly (for cheap thrills), or as a helpless victim (for signposts, as would be given over the phone to a potential rescuer).

"*HI bay*-beeeeeeeee! Oh my god, Farter just cleared out the checkout line at Safeway! You should see the looks I'm getting because of this fucking retard! Oh my god, Gene, it's horrible! Oh *bay*-beeeeeeeee, I'm getting all of my Christmas shopping done today with Farter! Please, I want you to come with me tomorrow for Christmas Eve!"

"With your family? Oh, I don't know, Bela."

"Oh pleeeeeeese, baby! They'll *LOVE YOU*! No, you have to wait until I'm off the phone! Remember what we just talked about at Burger King? Farter is fucking with my iPod, and he's got snot on his fingers. Oh BAY-BEEEEE! I'm coming over after work! I want you to fuck me in my tight little asshole, fuck it really rough and make me come like that!"

"Can't you get in trouble for talking like that in front
Of Fart-, I mean, your individual?"

"Anthony, do you want Gene to fuck my asshole?"

"Fuck fuck fuck," said Anthony.

"See?," said Izabela.

I didn't see at all, but I shuddered and sighed affectionately. I said goodbye and hung up. I began to dismantle what was left of my basement room setup and carry the file cabinets full of my writing, published and unpublished both, all of it, up the withered pine staircase and out of the crude stone and cinderblock cellar. Sam escaped deftly between my feet as I grappled with a five foot, 200 pound metal behemoth fit only for a scrap yard somewhere. By the time I noticed the massive bobcat in a blur of his ultra-fine, long yellow hair, he'd zeroed in on Alyosha, my spun-out housemate's male tabby. The beast had been slightly neglected by everyone, I believed, and he was as a result markedly withdrawn and timid in nature, so it must have been a peak negative experience for the diminutive fellow when Sam took him like a snowplow at top speed, and set upon him with such terrific violence that my heart skipped a beat, realizing then that each of Sam's paws were the size of

Alyosha's head, and that Sam's arms were throttling the small cat's torso. He was raising the entirety of Alyosha's small frame up and into the front door with a hateful and sickening point-of-impact "WHUMP", and I heard the air explode from his Alyosha's lungs. By this time, Sam's claws and teeth were deeply entrenched in cat- hide, and the majesty of him, all three feet of top predator demon-fire (with another foot of epically plumed tail) worked away, his eyes having flushed in an instant from sick-piss yellow to a hard obsidian, barely seeing at all. Gore spattered, and surrounded by enough loose fur to stuff a parka, and maybe a few teddy bears, Sam retreated from the spent and bloodied tabby only with a hard kick from one of my size 13 motorcycle boots.

"YOU. Little. Mother. FUCKER!"

Before the scene was finally over, I too would be lacerated from fingertip to wrist, and I would have him beside me on my mattress there in that dank cellar, our heads together, staring each other down, me fairly awestruck by the prolonged street cruelty and violence which had molded Sam, his fear and his hate. It was dawning on me, piecemeal style, that I would have to learn to be patient with Sam, and that I must do everything in my power to love this great and terrible specimen whom I pitied with great sadness and the knowledge of multiple sicknesses that were bigger than the sum of me and all I knew.

-6-
(dirty seasonal effects)

The drive to D.C. from Baltimore takes about 45 minutes, I'm told. On Christmas Eve, I wore a black sportscoat with an ugly purple dress shirt, my only "nice" shirt, underneath. Jeans and boots. Sloe-eyed. Greasy hair and a sloppy shave – toilet paper bits, and tufts of cat hair on my shoulders. Izabela beside me, behind the wheel. No snow. Fleetwood Mac on the radio.

Our first stop: her father, Ernest Slutzky.

Sitting there, I thought of the sweetness of past lovers who any decent man would have fled from, women who made the average man feel small, who dominated sexually, intellectually, or both. I'd never been afraid of these women, and, in their own ways, they had been good to me. They had been good to my cat.

I thought of Pam, a convicted murderer. She'd never eaten filet mignon, or been on a tropical vacation. She didn't know who or what Dolce Gabana was. She could not be called upon for a political discussion, or a trip to an art museum. She was a stupid little hick, and she'd killed another human being. But she was good to me. There were things we both knew, and knowing that the other knew just as well, *that* knowing always took away a degree of tension that makes people unable to live with or even visit other people. We had all that extra freedom and extra space in our heads that we could devote to caring about each other, if only for that moment. It's just that that moment kept happening.

Jackie spent her formative years being raped by her father, which she said turned her into a groupie during the early 1970s, a 12 year old demon swallowing rock star come in hotel rooms. She eventually made it so that I couldn't have fun anymore, and she was a cat killer. I could forgive her. In those days, I was very inexperienced, which meant a lot of screaming fits when I felt cornered, or estranged. She had to forgive me every night.

I thought of Sondra, with the 70cats. She never knew what day it was, but she took care of those cats. All of them obeyed her like dogs, and their litter boxes were always clean. The night I picked her up at a bar, along Eight Mile Road in Detroit, she had a dead kitten in the passenger seat of her Econoline van. She cruised the roads at night in that van, looking for places to dump her 200 pound bags of cat litter, and for strays who were lost in the cold. The dead kitten had a child's band-aid on its front leg, where an IV had been installed. The band-aid had little paw prints printed on it.

"She didn't make it," Sondra said. She was drunk.

"You don't mind, do you?"

I didn't mind. I held the kitten as though it were very much alive, all the way back to her house in Highland Park.

Suddenly, I realized that the only possible saving grace at this point would start with me throwing myself from this car at the next off-ramp, and walking back to Baltimore. I was fidgeting. Izabela made a smart-ass little cunt kind of a remark, and I kept my head pressed against the glass of the passenger window.

We pulled into the parking lot of a low-income housing project, and I got out with a bag of small gifts, and blowing steam in the freezing damp air, following behind my girlfriend, passing by clusters of people who, Izabela revealed, were Eastern European immigrants, the entire suburban ghetto back-lot being a cozy and bleak discount affair of Poles, Turks, Russians, and Slavs. These people –all men-- loitered, smoking heavily, without regard for the passing strangers. I like to catch other men in the act of scoping a girlfriend's ass, and Izabela's merited more than a scope, as much, in fact, as a surreptitious trawl around a supermarket, even a detour around the block… but I didn't give a good fuck who scoped her, on this day or any other. We approached the second or third building, in a series of many more: large concrete eyesores containing 6, 10, 12 units in each. Civilized, sensible, hard working people. Reasonable rates. Moribund.

A handsome, and sharply threatening man met us in a disinfectant-reeking, under-lit stairwell. His handshake said: MERCENARY. I thought of the photos and the stories. I almost heard him call me a "mudder-fucking peez ov shit" in my brain as I returned pressure with my own right mitt, in which all bones were already pulverized from my living room wall, a fearsome injury which had healed quite badly and would never be fixed in a proper manner. What he had actually said was pleasant and mundane, but I didn't buy it. I gave Ernest a well-rested, freshly shaven leer, overcompensating in response to his handshake, and also to Izabela's warnings about her dad's hyper- protective nature. She had been just as quick to educate me on his penchant for woman-beating. A hypocrisy, I thought, too incredibly stupid to bother pondering. But my first instincts assured me that Izabela's woman beating, ex-soldier, ex-mercenary, ex- cab driving Federal agent dad was, all things considered, a nice guy.

As we entered his cramped, tomblike apartment, I observed the presents, the artificial Christmas tree…it was a typical working class immigrant hovel. I felt some warmth there, and relaxed to the idea of being accepted by Ernest, and later, his estranged wife. Izabela's stepfather, a German immigrant she of course referred to as "the Nazi", might prove to be the bitch of the bunch. But I felt ready.

Immigrants are not boring to Americans, and their fierce loyalties are fascinating to us. To be accepted by her family was also to be entertained and inspired. It was a romantic hope, in strict accordance with my view of myself as a nation-less man, as full-flavored, 100- proof, unpatriotic heathen-scum. I was fully aware of this during our visit with Ernest, when we stuffed our faces with all manner of salty, lard-heavy Polish comfort food. Izabela's paternal grandmother emerged as we sat down to eat. She said nothing in English, and very little in Polish. The other granny, who lived with Izabela's mother and the Nazi, was completely batshit, I'd been told. But Ernest's mom wasn't the crispiest piece of toast on the sandwich either. She sat in a catatonic state, rousing only when I approached the bowl containing some type of creamed herring. She would murmur in Polish, and gesture for me to eat more. Ernest denied that the syrupy substance he served as a refreshment contained alcohol, but it was obviously a liqueur. The tablecloth was cheap plastic, and had a child's party "happy birthday" design pattern. The chairs were plastic, and the kitchen was hardly bigger than a walk-in closet. We were all smashed in there together.

Back in her clown car, Izabela explained that Ernest had thought more of me than her other boyfriends, a long series of flamboyant art students and fey indie rock Dorothies.

"I think he appreciates the fact that you act like you have a dick. You're confident, and manly," she said.

This kind of thing is never terrible to hear about oneself, especially when one has enough good sense to be powerfully disgusted by manliness, confidence, dicks, and all the rest of it. It's not your own pompous big dick bullshit you rage against in your heart. It's always everyone else's.

I was becoming smug and complacent with this small nod of approval, when Izabela started grinning at me.

"He knows you're an alcoholic, Gene."

"I thought you didn't say anything about that."

"I didn't, but-"

"And those drinks he gave us. That was booze. Why did he keep saying it wasn't?"

"Look, he doesn't think you're a bad person, but-"

"He swore up and down that the stuff wasn't alco-"

"It's not about the drinks, honey."

"I didn't drink before we got there. I didn't *stink* of anything."

"I know, but bay-beeeeee…"

Her horrible laughter filled the car.

"*Baybeee* WHAT?," I said.

Her putrid cackle intensified. She turned down the radio, and looked at me, pure delight dripping from her eyeballs.

She said:

"Oh baby. Your poor little hands were shaking the whole time!"

Suddenly, I remembered why people like Ernest beat their women. It was going to be a rough night.

Thirty minutes later, I found myself in a massive 3 or 4 million dollar ranch-style mansion, surrounded by people who all stank of money. I didn't know who was who, and didn't care, because it was such a hairy scene, so noisy with children and constant arrivals that no one could expect me to remember a name. A nice middle-aged man in a Polo shirt with a nice middle- aged wife in a double knit Christmas-themed sweater approached as we sat down on a leather davenport the size of a Cadillac. I shook their hands, and we exchanged Christmas words. The man offered me a beer, and he was quick to offer me another when I'd finished that one. The house was owned by the Nazi's sister. The Nazi was a grim-faced old German with a hateful sense of humor, and like Ernest, a history of violence toward women. He disliked me on sight. He and Izabela had hated each other for many years. I wondered if he knew that she called him "The Nazi".

For being The Nazi, he seemed like an intelligent man. He was of course extremely German, with the hard stare of an alcohol-scarred, misery-addicted misanthrope. Maybe he thought of *himself* as The Nazi. I normally try to like such people, and I'll defend them to their enemies even if I can't find anything to like. I didn't like anything about The Nazi, and I would never think to defend him. Still, I preferred his company to Izabela's. My girlfriend clung to me as a means of angering The Nazi, and I let her enjoy the act, returning her playful pinches and kisses. Her mother was a sweetheart, and you could tell that she'd once been pretty –to certain tastes, anyhow. Eastern European women have always been irresistible to me. A sharp, hooked nose is common in that region, with tough physical stances, and curled lips framing mouths that are joyless, and mighty legs, dark eyes that squint with derision, large asses that are evil/gorgeous but somehow angry. They are not delicate women, and they will plant a knife in you so much quicker than a woman from North Carolina or Japan or even Mexico. There is no violence as pure as the desperate, clean-killing efficiency of the Eastern Europeans. Vera Slutzky was a jocular, squat, and round-featured woman whom Izabela resembled strongly; she invoked in her plainness and warmth the peasant woman she had once been in Poland. She beamed at me, winking at

Izabela, while across the room The Nazi stood solemnly surveying all three of us. Something in me begged to know: would it be hot to fuck Izabela's mother? Oh yes, yes it would, I decided.

Then they announced dinner.

"It's fondue", Izabela whispered to me.

"What's fondue?"

She giggled her sub-normal 4 year-old giggle. "You don't know what fondue is?"

I was then dragged to a chair at a banquet table to which all 40 or 50 guests also flocked to ungraciously. I sat down in the chair, and before me was The Bottle: Nave del Fantasma.

For years, I'd eyed it contemptuously, angrily, lusting for it, in liquor stores all over the country. During the years 2005 and 2006, I'd managed to pull in a grand or so a week as a black marketer of unreleased and otherwise unavailable sex films. I sold these bootleg discs to fiending movie geeks around the globe, and the profits afforded me the opportunity to become something of a wine snob. But even then, during my tours of the local wine outlets, I never dared reach for a bottle tagged more than fifteen or twenty dollars. Nave del Fantasma was among those vintners whose complex-structured, medium or large bodied, $50 or $75 a pop ambrosias I promised myself I would taste if I could work that grand a week up to two or three times that.

But I never did. And I spent my money foolishly anyway, never having had money, so it didn't matter. In hindsight, I should have splurged, instead of constantly buying roses for dumpy middle-aged bar maids. But there it was: Nave del Fantasma, a 2003 Monastrell. I looked down both sides of the table, and every two or three seats down was another bottle. There were four bottles to my left, three to my right. I instinctively knew that I'd never have this chance again.

Izabela was explaining fondue to me. I nodded. When the Nave del Fantasma was offered to me, I sighed and nearly melted into my chair.

"Oh yes, of course."

I drank. And reeled. Cities raged, engulfed in firestorms. Its beauty was a hard slap in the face. Old women shrieked as their loved ones burned. Money meant nothing. It was anarchy.

"So you take the bread from here, and dip into – Gene!"

"Yeah. Ohhhhh. Oh, oh. God DAMN."

Virgin girls lined up in a ditch, black sky yawning, black rain pelting my back…

"Ohhhh. God DAMN."

"Gene!"

A small tight pinch at my ribs, Izabela's lips pursed.

Her voice became hushed. "You told me- listen!- you told me you can't drink wine on beer. You-HEY!-you TOLD me that every single time you get nasty. Please…"

"Iz, it's the fucking HAUNTED BOAT! Do you know-

"Shhh!"

"Do you know what's in that bottle? Holy fucking-"

Izabela's right hand swept under my shirt and her nails sunk into the skin of my left side.

"SHHH!"

"One glass," she said. "And that means *ghost ship*, not *haunted boat*. Fucking retard."

Nave del Fantasma, by the third sip, had reduced what I considered an informed palate to smoking rubble. It was far better than sex; certainly, it beat sex with Izabela.

During dinner, my enthusiasm never turned into a bona fide scene, yet those around me knew I was halfway to shitting myself with joy. It never dawned on them that it could be something as simple as good, classy wine. I was eager to pair the wine with food, and I deigned not to cool the scalding fondue before nipping it from my fork, burning the skin off my tongue every time. In an attempt to dull or distract myself from the pain, I slapped my hands together, muttering "fantastic!" and "hoo boy!" and "wow!"

The bottle in front of me drained, and my momentum strong, I winced at the realization that I'd have to ask for another. I did, and it was brought. Izabela had long since taken on an air of indifference. Shame began to sing in those pockets of my gut which were not swirling with the Monastrell. The Nazi no longer ate or drank, but simply stared, a dull-bull roar in his eyes, hoping that his life-energy would transcend physical reality and burn a hole in me somewhere. Then the plates and pots were taken away, and the table gathering was dismantled, as Izabela was coming to terms with having failed to disrupt my booze junkie's gravitational pull.

The daughters and cousins and mothers and uncles and foreign exchange students scattered, mostly to the living room and its Italian leather davenports and love seats. I glowed with enough alcoholic energy to power several Manhattan blocks, and I knocked back beer after beer, expensive German beers, losing sight and feeling of those ghosts which had visited me, of Hank and the pit bulls. I shook hands with four different foreign exchange students, and spoke to a girl of only five or six about the scars on my arms – now visible, with the removal of my outer shirt. She explained to me why I did this to myself, and I excitedly shared with Izabela my astonishment that this child could so eloquently define what I'd neglected to even consider all of these years.

Izabela rolled her eyes.

I had six beers in me, in addition to the wine, and the other beers, and my refills were beginning to appear with increasing delays. I was beyond drunk. I knew that more than one person here had noticed my guzzling; discernible to me also was their faint apprehension upon realizing that I would not Stop. Izabela smiled at me and said nice things. She wanted me to lose my composure and cause a scene. But I kept smiling and laughing and shaking hands and saying, "Merry Christmas" to these rich cocksuckers. One of the foreign exchange students was Polish, and for a time I forgot that Izabela –who spoke her native tongue fluently- was right next to me. I obeyed all rules, I kept my words innocuous and insignificant and dishonest, but we were flirting, the young Polish girl and I. We were flirting in all the usual speechless ways. I wondered if she was fucking the head of the house, the weasel in the Polo shirt, the Nazi's brother. I was certain that she was. I was also certain that she had fallen for me; her eyes begged me to save her from this pit of Hell. That poor dear. I wanted to rip her clothes off right then and there, in front of Izabela and The Nazi and everyone. I'd take her with me to Harrisburg, and make her my concubine, because I couldn't see any other way of getting better.

First though, I'd need a cigarette. I was seven beers in, going with the way of it all, going with Christmas and rich people and one Polish girl who was painfully unhappy with the stupid American rich people and another Polish girl who was watching my every move to determine exactly when and how I would blow my top and whatever was going to happen, it would have to wait, because I was eight beers in, and my teeth were sharp, and my wrists were still badly scarred, and it was time to smoke a fucking cigarette.

-7-

(real animal)

Muddy snow, barking dogs, a wide open boom of night shifting across the land, hundreds of half-million and million dollar houses, lost in a den of stinking riches, where all the good steaks and good bottles go, where men rape their maids and solicit their foreign exchange students, where incest happens boringly, everything one could guess correctly upon even a cursory examination, in these houses around us.

Izabela trudged along beside me, muttering and cursing. I was not reasonable about the red flags I'd already flown, the taunting of the bull Nazi, and I could not see how it was somehow gauche to palm a beer as we left the party and the house (our departure was itself less than polite) to drink during our walk to the nearest convenience store. Izabela had refused me the swiped bottle. I was only trying to keep myself in good cheer.

So without my bottle, I slipped into a dehydrated surliness, and we went our separate ways when a disagreement arose regarding the directions to the store. To the right went she, along the sludgy sidewalk, and I lost sight of her quickly. The four lanes of asphalt we'd crossed now buzzed brazenly with constant traffic. I turned to the left, where the road twisted, and began my walk into a dark stretch where I could plainly see that no gas stations or convenience stores stood. I walked anyway, the road continuing to snake, and I considered my money: $20. Possibly just enough for a bus back to Baltimore, but it couldn't have been earlier than 10 PM; I'd be sleeping in a Greyhound station under the best of circumstances, and the walk there could be ten miles or more. Maybe twenty. You're lucky to thumb a ride in the country, but in a D.C. suburb the best you can hope for is to not get picked up by the police for vagrancy.

I stacked the benefits of my escape plan against these awfully harsh drawbacks. Obviously, I wouldn't have to fend against the smoldering hatred of the Nazi, or stiffen up with nerves over his eventual full-frontal assault in plain sight of countless strangers, most if not all of whom had already begun to suspect me of degeneracy. And it would simply *have* to be the end of Izabela and I.

Good things, all. But that cold marathon walk, that bus station hangover morning…I'd had too many hells like that. It was my pre-maturely old bones I thought of, not the worth of the discomfort, but of course it *would* have been worth it. I could then return to the original plan, to the warming knowledge of a clean break from "The Greatest City In America", formerly "The City That Reads". (Baltimore proclaimed this to the rest of the nation, in their tourism pamphlets and commercials, during my years there. It was stenciled on their public benches. To me, Baltimore's attempts to transform its own national identity seemed to surpass the stupendously asinine, veering from idiocy into flagrant self-neglect, possibly even masochism…a lot like that snot-licking, ass-scratching, sexually abused child in second grade whose humiliating behavior only worsened as his peers' laughter escalated. And as with that poor child, whom I did not dramatically differ from at the time, I could not bring myself to feel pity for Baltimore.)

My mind shooting half-dead burnout sparks, I continued my walk, resting occasionally in a snowdrift, sandwiched between the road and someone's high picket or chain- link fence, the urgency of my mistake in leaving Izabela growing with every footfall. It seemed I'd gone over a mile; there would be no finding her now. And it wouldn't matter I did: she was not one to grovel or apologize first.

I began to rise from my third drop-off spot, intending to ignore logic and continue my forward stomp, when there was a hateful punch upon the opposite side of the fence, against which my back still pressed. This was followed by a series of oafish barks, and wet snarls.

The pit bulls in Baltimore were declared "not vicious" by

the courts. They -dogs, that is- all seemed vicious to me, not least the American Staffordshire Bull Terrier, a/k/a *pit bull*. I was immediately to my feet and moving, back towards Izabela, and what I now understood was the correct direction if I wanted to smoke. The dog's foaming rage dimmed behind me, and within 10 minutes I found her, sitting at a bus stop bench, in tears. I knelt before her, and told her I was sorry.

"The Nazi just texted me. He says you better slow down. He says he'll call the cops on you."

"Alright," I said, grumbling internally at her mention of "texting".

"We still have to go to midnight mass," she said.

"Alright."

"The gas station's just down the road. Let's get your cigarettes."

"Alright, Izzy."

"Iz," she said.

"What?"

"Don't call me Izzy. For the hundredth fucking time."

"Alright. Do you love me?"

"Yeah, Gene. Let's go."

We began walking. She wasn't such a horrible girl. She was walking with me. Maybe she was trying to understand me, and maybe she was waiting for me to show her something I'd failed to thus far. But I knew not to wait for her. I could only try to be kind, because I had bruises that needed healing, and my juicehead fuck-brain told me that only a woman with whom I was sexually involved held the potential of facilitating this process. I needed to be put away somewhere. But I didn't even have a woman to help me. All I had was a little girl. Well, mostly little. Silence settled on us as we approached an intersection, and the 25-pump fill-station which teemed with idling SUVs, tractor trailers, clown cars like Izabela's, all manner of gas-guzzling douche-wagons. The cold was getting to her, and I fully anticipated an attack on the way home. I made my foolish purchase, Marlboro Reds, and eagerly extracted the first of the cigarettes with numb fingers and severe respiratory difficulty. I never could handle my nicotine, and defined myself as a non-smoker, yet I always seemed to be smoking. I am dreadfully afraid of cigarette smoke, of what it does to the body and what the habit itself says about the user, yet I was never without a pack of cigarettes.

After Hank's killing, what haunted me most was my ignorant tendency, during all of those 14 years with him, to fill the many apartments we shared with smoke, always being too drunk to consider the ill effects and discomfort of the oxygen killing cyanide fumes on the mind and body of a small animal. It was that for which I hated myself most. This hatred invaded my thoughts, and I gave in there, walking through a field, during a shortcut back to the main road, shin-deep in snow, I gave in to the bottom line which was that I deserved to be killed, preferably by the same pit bulls, for what I'd allowed to happen to my cat.

Izabela –for reasons known only to her- began at that very moment a personal attack on me as a writer.

"Crime fiction isn't *real* literature, you know," she said, and "what you're doing is just this kind of Bukowski trash, that whole 'I'm a drunk' thing!", she said, and then, "I'm going back to school to take more writing courses, because I'm a *real* writer," and then, "does *your* novel have a beginning, a middle, and an end? REAL books, by REAL writers, all have a beginning, a middle, and an end!"

I wondered if I should forgive her. God knows, the things that come out of my mouth under the influence are more often than not absolutely, categorically *un*-forgivable, yet I always seem to be forgiven. I said nothing as we neared the edge of the field, tractor trailers and their roaring by now quite distant from us, the filling station sparkling and flashing behind us, when I noted that she did not seem to be drunk at all, and that I had heard quite enough from her, so I shoved her to the ground and began dragging Izabela by her feet closer to the roadside.

"I'm going to throw you under one of those trucks," I announced with clenched teeth. "You stupid fucking brat, I'll show you what I'm capable of! I've got nothing to lose now, you miserable fucking cunt!"

Izabela screamed and thrashed and threatened me with police, but no one could hear her pitiful, grotesque wailing except me. I got her as far as the sidewalk, as one lone truck sprayed us both with mud and salt. Her screams became ferocious; she was fighting for her life, and pleading for it. My foot became lodged in the ground, probably the entrance to a hedgehog's lair. I stumbled and collapsed, my foot still submerged. I released Izabela and sat there wishing I was a hedgehog as she delivered a series of hard kicks to my back and ribs. Headlamps glanced off our coats and our frosty hair, as I caught one more kick to the balls which left me slack jawed and whimpering softly. She spit in my eyes, and shrieked, "I'm going to tell my father about you! My father will fucking kill you, piece of shit! He has friends who hunt terrorists! What do you think they'll do to a piece of shit like you?"

My teeth no longer chattered, because I couldn't feel anything but my half-ruptured testes. I saw tires down there, and some grass, and some rocks. I stared up at the sky, and watched the snow falling. I remained there until Izabela returned and helped me regain my footing upon the grass, then upon and onward across the frozen shelf of sidewalk.

"You can't drink any more! Don't you get it? The Nazi hates you, he's on to you! We still have to go to midnight mass!"

We walked and walked, perhaps a half mile until the turn off to the Nazi's family's house. My head pulsed with dehydration and hypothermia. It seemed I'd been out there in the field a long time before she came back. I wondered how midnight had not passed. Perhaps it had. There'd be hell to pay if we were late for midnight mass.

I noticed a large metal structure at the edge of the woodland, two blocks away from our mansion, a kind of power-base which appeared to be the device that controlled the stoplights or maybe the streetlights there. It was almost large enough to hide two adult human bodies. Izabela was sobbing and I began to feel remorse for what I had done, but the remorse, combined with her heaving chest and smeared makeup, must have turned me on a little, because before I could reason with myself, or understand what I was doing, I had dragged her down the embankment and behind the warm, humming power box which I slammed her into with such force that the streetlights fluttered briefly on and off while I yanked down her skirt and leggings and forced myself up her ass viciously from behind.

She did not put up a very strong fight, and although tears streamed down her cheeks, she was keeping a hate-fuck kind of rhythm with me; and whether it was the possibility that our heads and faces were completely visible to passing cars, or that I was probably hurting Izabela, I decided that this course of action was unnecessarily reckless, and immediately began mentally transposing the suburban DC winter setting to some ramshackle approximation of suburban winter Krakow, and Izabela as a troublesomely young girl there, who I'd happened upon in an innocent enough fashion during a stroll home from my job at the local steel factory. The notion of her diminutive body, left torn and heaving there in the snow…that did it for me, and then it was done, leaving us both free to complete the trek home. No words were spoken, but when we approached the front door of the house, I could see that her sobbing had only escalated. I was prepared to run, and leave my "luggage" as it were behind.

I wasn't any more eager to be murdered at that moment than I'd been an hour ago, and Izabela did have a penchant for petulance, tantrums, phony shrieks of terror, bogus cries for help, the objective being the scourging of the gentleman, any gentleman, who dared to openly challenge or insult her, by any chivalrous passerby. I simply did not understand chivalry, to whatever degree it was genuinely practiced as a general rule in this heathen age, but regardless of all notions thereof, what a bone-chilling display had already been enacted, on several occasions, when she tired of my sloppy social performances.

At a party the week before, she'd thrown her drink in my face, and immediately voided her lungs of air with a Circean slash of such aural violence that I'd had to cover my ears. This act brought my disconcerting and wilted presence sharply into the focus of nearly a dozen bristling young men, all zeroing in on a perfect opportunity to plunder Izabela's rank little dream box. I have to admit, I was terrified: the more feminine these young Muppets appear, the more ferocious their swings; they fight like drag queens, which is to say dirtily and at any necessary length.

And there we were, away from Baltimore's many threats, but at critical mass with the Nazi already on the verge of murder. If she began such a routine for his benefit, I'd be sure to lose all of my front teeth, at best. I liked my teeth. They needed quite a bit of work, and were painfully decalcified, but I did not want to die toothless. I began edging away from her and the door, still only scant feet away from either, when there was a shout:

"THEY'RE BACK! Jesus CHRIST!"

I was pounded by an explosion of light and Izabela spun away from it, into a shadowed portion of the marble porch, as I simply froze. The Nazi burst through the door, as if he had been leaning forward against it at a 90 agree angle with the floor when it opened (no matter that the door opened inward). My freshly kicked nut sack, hanging limp and petrified, still managed to ascend into my body cavity as he tore straight past me, cursing in short bursts, as if straining at full sentences and not finding them, and resorting to physical tremors. He threw himself behind the wheel of a gas-guzzling douche-wagon, only inches from our knees, and barked, not just to me or to Izabela, but several others who now filed through the door, in that golden shaft of electric light, out into the cold:

"WELL LET'S GO! CHRIST'S SAKE! LATE! EVERY FUCKING- AND DIDN'T I FUCKING SAY- NOW! LATE! LET'S GO!"

I was in an SUV then. I was sitting next to Izabela, and my lips were cracked, and I was severely dehydrated, crashing from the righteous shock of alcoholic electricity, of pain and fear and roadside sodomy. Izabela began laughing and talking to everyone but me, and although the Nazi had not seen her tears (certainly concealed intentionally by Izabela, for she was never observed in any condition she did not intend to be observed in, her character in any case being altogether venal), he was quick to remark, with a bitter disgust in his voice,

"It SMELLS like a BREWERY in here!"

He shook his head all the way to the church, and I dared

not glance up into the rearview mirror, for I knew what I would find there. Nor did I speak to the other passengers, two middle aged men and two   middle-aged women, all reasonably   healthy-looking, kind and chattering softly, everything soft with them. I did not remember their names, which was to be expected. It did trouble me that their faces, also, did not register in my mind. I told myself that these individuals had arrived after Izabela and I's excursion, but I knew they had not.

At   the   church, which was the size and general shape of a Wal-Mart store, we cruised past a parking lot the size of a drive-in movie theater, with no parking spaces to be found. We continued along a dirt road, some 50 yards past the parking lot, and found a spot there. The moon gleamed down, bright and full, hoot owls and the dead electric hum of middle-of-nowhere power lines, as we crunched across the tundra. It was a long and silent walk back to the church, where several thousand Christians made entry difficult. We had to stand at the back, and even then, in rows. I was getting scowled at by many of them.

It was well after midnight now, and was I really to believe, blindly and affectionately, that none of these people were drunk? Didn't they work jobs that induced in them such hellish sadness that drug habits and transvestisism and sadomasochism lurked menacingly in the periphery of their lives? Didn't they peep on their own sons and daughters and fuck their best friends' wives and husbands? Certainly they were not above a couple of cocktails on Christmas Eve. The Nazi, just to the left of me, mumbled something under his breath about little boys being forced to fellate priests, and Izabela, just to the right of me, started giggling. We were all thinking the same things, but we hated each other most of all. Thinking about this gave me a stomach cramp, so I went outside to smoke and fart. When I reached the front of the church, several young men were standing there as if in waiting for me. They gave me a stare of contempt that did laps around the Nazi's burning orbs, and I went into denial instantly. The threat of physical violence, from Izabela, Izabela's aspiring future suitors, the Nazi, or any number of others, was omnipresent, and had visited upon me so much dread and despair that I had finally reached a point of defiance, but not in the sense of standing up to anyone. I'd simply ignore them, and resort to fists and feet and teeth only if attacked first. I consider myself a reasonable man, and these people were Christians.

I lit my cigarette, and one of the young men skipped across the church's vast, yawning face with such deliberation that he seemed to float, as well Jesus might have, across the water, and he spat:

"HEY! Listen you goofy motherfucker, there's no SMOKING out here. Why don't you just go back to the BAR?"

Oh, they were on to me. And I felt sorry for the young lads; well, perhaps not these two specifically, but the many others whom I'd angered by coming here tonight, who had been true Christians, and kept their traps shut.

I backed away from him, into a cluster of trees which adjoined the church's north side (although it may have been the east, or south, or west side) and sucked into my cigarette, full of fear, vanishing through the trees, and making a light, jaunty sprint all the way around the church back to the starting point, which took several minutes.

When I'd arrived again at the entrance, the Christian boys were gone, and I returned to the warmth and assurance of my companions inside. I now reeked of tobacco and alcohol both, and stood there for two consecutive hours, groping Izabela and listening to the hymns and the carols. My legs were hurting, all stiffness and numbness, and drooping /itchy eyes, and anxiety, general fatigue...I think it was the same for everyone else, too, it just had to be, but for me particularly. People began to file out, shuffling like one of Izabela's retards, which we did also.

I woke up later that night, with Izabela fast asleep next to me, and snuck out the window of the large mansion. I dropped down onto one roof, which made me practically piss myself with fear and humiliation, thinking I'd be caught and having no answer for my discoverers. But no one came. I dropped down from that roof onto the frozen ground, landing in something that may or may not have been excrement. I padded gently back out onto the main road, turning right, past the big power box and back to the filling station, where I bought a gallon of antifreeze and a lukewarm hotdog. Crossing the field once again, I laid my purchases beside me on the ground.

First, I tried to imagine what might happen if Izabela were to awaken and find me missing. I suspected that absolutely nothing would happen, because if she had intended on giving me up to the Nazi, she would have done so already. He had given me a very stern warning about leaving my room to smoke or forage for more alcohol in his brother's kitchen. Before drifting off to sleep, Izabela confided that the Nazi had advised her to find another boyfriend.

"Someone not so hard," he said. "Someone not so...old."
I thought briefly about screwing Izabela in the ass. She was all I had, but I knew I was not in love with her, and would never be. Was I just laying here, thinking about screwing Izabela, because I didn't want to keep walking?

The ice was burning into my lower back, where my t-shirt and coat had slipped above my waist. I walked out of the field, hit the sidewalk, past the big power box, past the bench where Izabela had sat, waiting for me when I'd gone left instead of right. I passed the turn-off to Izabela and the Nazi and kept going. I found a snowdrift with a huge crater in it, which sloped down along a chain link fence. I slid down against it with my bag of treats, and I waited and I listened.

Book Two

HARRISBURG NOCTURNITIS

-8-

(guantanamo-on-the-susquehanna)

Izabela and I returned to Baltimore in silence, and all remained silent for a couple of days, until it dawned on me that I had no driver for the U-Haul. I coughed up the requisite apologies, and prepared a large dinner of T-bone steaks with a 1.5 liter bottle of Concha Y Toro's bottom rung Cabernet, which had been a big hit with me that week. We went on walks through the Northwest Baltimore ghettos at night, Christmas ennui and frozen squalor. I bare-knuckled her to several climaxes underneath my duct-taped sidewalk transom windows, and took her to see a Scottish film, a comedy about teenage abortion, at the Charles Theater, where they had still forgotten to officially fire me, and where we witnessed a crawling sex pervert attempt to fellate a woman's toes in the next row during the film's second reel. The woman reacted as if cattle-prodded; she began gnashing her teeth and shrieking like a baboon. Izabela smacked me in the nose when she realized I was chuckling to myself. They had to stop the movie and bring up the houselights. I knew the man was harmless; I'd dealt with him many times before, sympathetically, of course. Now, with my indeterminate status as a staff-member, the Charles had once again become vulnerable to sex beasts. Its management had no other imposing male presence to install in the lobby for this purpose.

(Many years ago, as a teenager, I'd permitted a scrawny black chicken-queen to lick my engineer boots in a bus station men's room; what business was it of mine if someone wanted to suck toes or lick boots, especially if it brought them such a profound happiness? I suppose it brought me happiness too; after all, it was a selfless gesture, and I really don't think of others often enough. None of us do, if you want to be truly honest about it.)

Then it was time to rent a U-Haul truck. It took about an hour to load the awful god damn thing, and with the bobcat now docile from fear, perched stiff and trembling upon my lap, and Izabela gloating furiously, showing off her relative prowess in maneuvering the behemoth through traffic or between as pumps, and a promise to leave alcohol alone, and Fleetwood Mac once again on the radio, I was so happy to be leaving Baltimore I could have wept.

Hitting a plastic pint of Popov surreptitiously with corn chip breath chasers during the 90 minute drive to Harrisburg, I made a point not to think about our destination.

Between my Harrisburg of 1996, and my Harrisburg of now, in the ugly mid-winter of 2009, there had been so many cities that I'd lost track of them all. And today, rumbling and rolling and slamming about behind me in the 12 foot U-Haul was a large assemblage of mostly scavenged items from Detroit and Baltimore curbside trash piles. In that 13 year interim, all I'd managed to hold onto was my Hungarian grandmother's writing desk, and a bare aluminum spatula. These items first came to me in the fall of 1995, when my marriage to a 15 year old high school student dissolved and I went flailing into bachelorhood, via the homosexual nightlife of downtown Harrisburg (I worked both the Harrisburg hospital emergency room and the YMCA front desk graveyard shift).

I had spiraled into degradation and self-abuse via a disintegrating rear-efficiency apartment, 2nd floor, on 2nd Street, 2nd and Forster to be exact, where I could not make it a block at the age of 18 without catcalls and exhortations from boisterous old queens.

Every night at the hospital: gunshot victims. And every night at the Y: all manner of scum-ridden misconduct, from teenage boys to women to dope deals to gay orgies, and I took the money, I took small bribes and large bribes, I kept my head down and said nothing. I collected as much as an extra hundred every week. Sometimes, I used the cash to send roses to my ex-wife. I had to stop sending the flowers when I was visited by a city police officer with a restraining order. A week after that, from a mean-spirited lawyer, came a decree-of-divorce. "Gene Gregorits, defendant. Jamie Riley, plaintiff." I knew I would never see her again.

In 1996, I never slept. The hospital was infested with spiders: large wolf spiders, hairy, fat, fast-moving spiders in nests the size of big-screen Sony Trinitrons, which I ruptured with broom handles every morning. At night, I smoked cigarettes and drank coffee and beer at the YMCA, I built a pointless physique doing chin ups on the sandstone door frames of the YMCA's gothic and spectral lobby, which would fill up with early morning river mist and the electric hum of its security system. Ruined men visited me there, and I saw my future in their ruddy complexions and romantic homosexual yearnings and prostitution and crack pipes.

In the morning, I went to the hospital and killed a few thousand spiders. Police would rap on the Plexiglas windows of the security booth, in which I would doze, they would slam the grid iron at the YMCA with their flashlights, and they would bark like dogs. They would make remarks about me to my face, and they would threaten to have me fired. The police would use obscenities and racial epithets, and I would be taken to interrogation rooms and coerced, I would be harangued and browbeaten by the police, inches from a suspect, a shooting, or drug death, or a statutory rape, and I would point my finger at him, and I would say, "yeah, he's the one," and then they would arrest him.

In 1996, I never slept. Morning would come slowly, and walking home from work, the great yellow sun would burn through me, I would be acidic from coffee and insomnia, I would be true-yellow, wired like fuck, and I would go home and read my mail beside the filter top litter box in my large, old, and mostly empty kitchen. The women who saw my classified ads in small magazines and wrote me letters were the only women in my life; they sent me dirty panties and collage artwork. I read their letters, and coasted from one fixation to the next. My letters were full of bile and angst and invariably frightened the women away.

I ate out of boredom, YMCA vending machine chow, Oscar Meyer, and coughed everything back up, pure acid. I sat by the river and started taking blades to myself at night. Razors. Steak knives. Broken beer bottles. It was too soon for me to see how my wife had been unfit for me, and how I was unfit for anyone. I was too close to it, and I simply screamed for her to come back. I didn't stop screaming for a year, and then I was a fully formed death dwarf, badly scarred from head to foot: I took my act on the road.

Cleveland. Tampa. Philadelphia. Bangor. Boston. Detroit. Baltimore. Newark. Columbus. Pittsburgh. Atlanta. Harrisburg.

Years later, I found that I could not stop fantasizing about a post-nuke Harrisburg. The tragedy of that intolerable sewer had remained a toxic element in my dreaming, and in my waking life.

I romanticized my invisibility there among all of those vagrants, and the daytime business people who flooded the restaurants during lunchtime. It was as if I had been secreted away there by a powerful force, or forces, that my squalid teenage purgatorio would bleed further and further out, into my 20s, or my 30s. I thought of my life in 1996 as a sacred mistake: the Church of the Abandoned Christ. There was so much I didn't know, vast worlds I had not touched and did not expect to ever touch in the future. Completely un-socialized and uneducated, I could not do anything normally, or even at all. I could not file tax returns, or drive an automobile, or ask out a woman, or drink in a bar. I could not go on vacation or cook or write or play a guitar or dance. I took refuge in books from my youth, "black novels" like *Naked Lunch* and *Last Exit to Brooklyn*. I'd kept the stereo from my marriage, and listened to rock'n'roll at night, drinking malt liquor, submerged in that kind of rural, lower class teenage misery that finds solace in moronic punk records and splatter films. None of my friends were literate, and I was consistently arrogant and snide to anyone my own age, aching for a conversation about William Burroughs or existentialism, about Marlon Brando or Charles Manson or the Sex Pistols, conversations that were out if my reach and which I subconsciously knew I wasn't equipped to sustain anyway.

I also knew that other men my age were driving cars, and having relationships, and talking about books. They did not go to movies alone, thinking about the Church of the Abandoned Christ and how this American city or that American city was somehow charged with Satanic energy. They did not ride the Greyhound buses alone, while writing letters to strangers from classified ads, theorizing about the city's provocation of an infernal masochism that would in time blossom as romantic genius. But I did these things. These things were keeping me alive, steaming in me, slow but steady, dragging me from one day to the next.

I paid my electric bills on time with post office money orders, did my grocery shopping in the suburbs with my father during weekends or evenings, and cursed the river while haunting back alleys at night. I felt the sharp sting of remorse for what I had put my parents through, and was unable to say very much to them. No one knew what to say to anyone. Sometimes, I would call my mother late at night, drunk on potent malt liquor, and she would ask me who was buying me alcohol.

The major streets of Harrisburg ran straight north and south, parallel to the river. There were multi-lane streets, and the speeding yuppies in their sports cars seemed to use them as racetracks: Front Street, Second Street, Third Street. With its many small valleys and steep hillsides and stone-arch bridges, and the river of course, you might picture a small-scale Pittsburgh. But Pittsburg is a friendly town.

In Harrisburg, after 5 o'clock, the attractive young women who worked in the office buildings would flee back to the suburbs. It became a ghost town. That's when the rats began creeping out:

Sad, ghoulish,

East Coast brutality.

Petty filth.

Casual dying. The walking dead, informing with their deaths all of the mausoleum whispers the YMCA was haunted by at night, and strangers picking up the signals I shot out, all intent and all doubt spilling from my pores.

I see myself walking from the hospital to the Y, the river and cars roaring past, gay men lurking in doorways, and a procession of cars, cruising like bored piranhas, following the pulse of the homosexual kingdom, that pulse which, if traced back in a trail of cough syrup haze, or by the pervert vibe, using the compass of some sick fuck's cocaine erection, would lead to the heart of this desolate, brutal town.

Harrisburg 1994: I lived uptown, with the Riley family, the only white family on the block. My wife's parents were dysfunctional, and she had been rebelling against them in her defiant meetings with me, on benches high atop the Susquehanna, riverside benches which caught the unsparing gales of wind, and turned our hands numb as we fumbled in each other's pants, both of us virgins, with rats rustling in the bushes and splashing in the January river below.

1994: future in-laws shrewdly contained the problem (because I would have stolen her from them otherwise): they made me part of the family.

We were married at the edge of the world, the Uptown Shopping Center: a crack-ravaged territory which seemed to be the only barrier between the city and some horrible infinite, a metaphysical void where spectral homeless men raped other spectral homeless men, where crippled old freight trains stood abandoned; like a cosmic wilderness that swirled angrily on the other side of China Wok Express, Jimmy the Hot Dog King, Beer World, Sav-A-Lot; and then, there, for us, the District Justice of the Peace, where WE were married and THEY were arraigned. It might have been romantic, but for Debbie and Bill, the in- laws, who insisted upon bearing witness to our marriage and to whom my wife would always defer.

We had no friends and our sex was abysmal. I worked as the dairy manager in an inner-city supermarket, eating up the profits and stealing with both hands. On my 2nd or 3rd day, I was on the grease-crusted floor of aisle 6, stocking cans of Bartlett pears. A teenaged black girl approached me, and without a greeting, began her solicitation: "MAN, you wan' a CAT?" The black girl and I ducked the paranoid stare of our string bean supervisor, a balding middle-aged nebbish (who later fired me for stealing cat food). We leapt from a loading dock into the back alley where we sprinted to her family's home, a cramped 2 bedroom apartment that smelled of wet Cheerios and urine, and I discovered him there, on a child's bed, asleep: Hank. I fell in love with him on sight. He would be adored and pampered by myself and the Riley family.

Two years later, he would prowl the back alleys unsupervised, coming and going freely through a window by the fire escape. Hank sometimes disappeared for several days, and I came to rely on his instincts, for I was in over my head with two full time jobs and indisposed with demons. It happened slowly, but a partnership was forged between the cat and I, and it was this that returned to me like a shot as Izabela took the last exit before the river, coasting off Route 81 and into the city of Harrisburg, Pennsylvania at 10 PM. I saw that the hospital was gone, and a new one had been built. I saw my old apartment, the building now empty and condemned. I saw the YMCA, and the capital building, the newspaper plant, the cold London-like back alleys that always made me think of Jack the Ripper, and other places that I had turned into myth by then.

In Jarretsville, Maryland, in a pasture behind a poorly kept farmhouse, Hank rested in an unmarked grave.

I was home, and it couldn't have made less sense.

-9-
(captivity)

My mother met us in front of the address, berating me for my tardiness as if Izabela wasn't there. "Just for once in your life, can't you do something normally, can't you act like an adult?" She fawned over the girl when I had been made sufficiently aware of the great inconvenience I'd caused her, of her long workday and age and family troubles. My brother, who lived around the corner arrived then, also in a foul mood. Although I'd pleaded with my mother to locate me a cheap room in a bad part of town, to make it easier for me to keep up with rent after I was settled and employed, she quickly realized it would be far easier to simply call Mike, with his buddies who dabbled in real estate to boost their already gargantuan salaries, and place me in the first overpriced downtown unit that became available.236 North Street was a shabby brick building, conjoined on either side with other apartment houses. The neighborhood, with its narrow streets, small cafes, and alleys, was familiar to me. Two blocks away was the Y, and the river, and my previous dwelling from 1996 where I'd first lived with Hank. Mike owned an entire house, with a stainless steel refrigerator, leather sofas, Italian teak and French oak everywhere, right around the corner. During my four month stay, he would not visit me a single time.

We had a few drinks at my brother's posh digs, where Izabela openly insulted him with remarks such as, "I am an artist, and a writer, an intellectual, really, so for me, sports are very offensive!" She kept her trademark sneer burning into him at high heat, and he stared knowingly at me in response, as if I had coached the brat. Leaving that sour scene soon after, Mike doubled parked the U-Haul in front of 236 North Street and we began the job. My brother told me in no uncertain terms that he had a bad back and shouldn't be lifting anything. I told him to go home, if that was the case, and let me continue on my own. "It won't be a problem," I insisted, as a demon blast of river air pummeled him in his sleeveless Philadelphia Eagles tank top, managing even to muss his thick, short, mousse encrusted hair. He shook his head at me as if I were afflicted with Down's Syndrome, grabbing a large metal file cabinet that required two men, then stomping into the cramped building's narrow entrance. All the while, he moaned like a wounded war hero on a stretcher. Mike, who stood only 5"5', was also crippled by a wide variety of complexes related to his height. To compensate, he lifted weights and got tribal tattoos. He spoke in a false baritone, always louder than necessary. He gave high fives, flashed his pearly whites while talking about his last bowel movement, and nearly broke your hand when he shook it.

Izabela and my mother were talking in the bedroom, and I stood in the front, staring down at the parked U-Haul. I looked around, and felt myself shrink as a perfect clarity sank into me: my job prospects were grim. At $650 a month for this rat hole, I was not only being fleeced, I was lining the pockets of Mike's slumlord crony, and probably Mike's pockets too. Both my brother and his partner had the look of men who were veteran date rapists, and performed "Dutch ovens" on their girlfriends when drunk. I'd paid the same rent living in New York City, a town where I'd been able to find work.

Of course, I hadn't been facially disfigured in those days. And those days were 13 years ago. I was approaching middle age, and I didn't know what to do about it. The apartment was a cruel, rugged little cell, uncomfortably tight, low ceilinged, punishingly whitewashed. The hallway was three feet long, and the "kitchen" was tucked into one side of the hallway. I knew I would only drink liquor and commit suicide there.

Now, were this a town with even a faint glow of mystery, or beauty, or culture, or intelligence, or kindness, I imagine my time there could have been less nauseating. If it were a town with hipster dive bars, vegan diners, used bookstores, and bicycle shops, the $650 rent would be easy to justify. Independent restaurants and shops to work in would make my autonomy possible. For years, I'd been filling out applications with larger companies, even corporations, out of desperation. Corporations who now used a monolithic background check agency of dubious Constitutionality to screen out undesirables, deviants, and subversives such as myself, using all the power afforded such an entity by billion dollar contracts with international retailers and eateries who are tired of wasting time and money hiring deadbeats, drunks, and eccentrics with nowhere else to go for a paycheck.

Of course, I've never gotten a call back. Not from Wal-Mart, or Appleby's, or Blockbuster. Not from anyone. I'd been living in the gutter too long, and somehow, They knew. And even the most militant, adventurous entrepreneurs in Harrisburg were so utterly without creativity that they used their corporate counterparts as business models, right down to the employee uniforms and decoration. No smart conversations, no chance of any self-affirmation, no cash; I wouldn't even be able to get laid in this town.

After 30 minutes, the large items were unloaded, and my brother vanished without a goodbye. My mother had spent this time applying newly purchased sheets and blankets to my bed: "I want you to take care of these things! I am not made of money!"

"Mom, I have my own sheets and blankets. I didn't need this stuff." My mother grimaced and glared with disgust:

"Everything you own smells like a damp basement! You are done living like some kind of sewer rat! You're going to stop drinking and act like a man for once!"

With that, she hugged me and left with an air of despondence and defeat. I installed Izabela in my menacingly small bathroom, about 2 feet by 2 ½ feet, with Sam, who was exhibiting signs of fatigue and panic in alternating bursts.

The cream-colored beast placed on her lap, so as to be calmed, and removed from the clatter of the hauling which remained, and with Izabela's gap-toothed smile fading behind me, I returned to the truck, grabbing two 50 pound boxes of books. I was not in shape, far from it in fact, nor had I been fed, and my legs buckled. I went down hard on one knee, and my mouth formed around a scream that would not come, as my throat seemed to clamp shut on it in convulsive terror. The pain was such that my face went white and I instantly broke out in a cold, clammy sweat, flat on my back between the back of the U-Haul and the front bumper of a BMW. I stared up at the night sky for what seemed like an hour, and, using the U-Haul as support, for fear of setting off the BMW's alarm (and this took some doing, because the truck was by my feet, requiring me to wriggle and squirm like a half- stomped cockroach there in the bowels of that wretched city in order to reverse my position), I was able to return to my feet. I had no sooner gained footing when the screaming began.

It was Izabela. I was not able to walk, but I walked anyway, pulling myself inch by inch with my palms flat along the stained white walls of the first floor hall, then up two flights using a wobbly handrail which I broke. In the bathroom, Izabela's face had also gone white, and she held up her right hand. I sputtered through a blaze of blinding hot pain, "what happened?"

"He bit me! Oh, it's BAD!"

"Let me see."

"I think I need to see a doctor. Oh it hurts! Gene…"

"Let me see."

Tears ran openly down her cheeks; she was frightened more than hurt, but the wounds were considerable. Izabela's hand was marked by four bloodless, already inflamed holes, black in the center; punctures that were probably bone-deep. I'd sustained the same injuries from Sam, and knew that even without the risk of toxoplasmosis, the healing process would be slow and painful for Izabela. And I told her this, with an apology.

"What did you do?"

"What did I DO? I didn't DO anything! ASSHOLE!"

Her sobbing became unbearable for me. She looked like a retarded child who had just dropped her ice cream cone: "I HATE THAT FUCKING CAT! HE'S MEAN! HE'S A HATEFUL FUCKING ASSHOLE PIECE OF SHIT!"

I dumped both rubbing alcohol and hydrogen peroxide on the wounds, and put her to bed. ("I'm sorry, honey, but that hand won't be good for very much for a while. I love you, baby. We'll soak it tomorrow.")

Another dozen heavy boxes remained on the truck. It took

me four hours, and a lot of cursing, to transport them to apartment 8. By the time I'd finished, Izabela had roused from a fitful nap and wanted a shower, but, of course, the landlord had turned off both the heat, and the hot water. She looked so pitiful and beleaguered laying there, her face grim and her words terse, that my contempt vanished on the spot. I began filling every pot I could find with water and boiling it on my miniature stove. But as soon as one pot had been dumped in the tub for her, the previous hot water had gone cold. By the time I filled the tub, it was 4 A.M. and Izabela had gone to sleep again. Sam was curled up beside her, purring. As I glanced at him, he began to yawn, big and wide, then slamming his jaws shut with a wet snap that reminded me of a crocodile. I scooped him up and carried him to the front room, where I made a bed for him in an empty box. I picked up the cushioned box and placed it back beside the girl. I stood there a while, watching the two of them. I'd gotten another pint of vodka from my laundry bag, and was under the impression, once again, that Izabela was not so bad.

But Izabela's bath was now ice-cold, and my contentedness proved to be very fleeting indeed. I was spitting mad, and beyond the point of caring whether or not things ever worked out for me, even little things. I went to Front Street with my cracked kneecap and a pack of Marlboros, and sat there above the river during a snowstorm for a while thinking of suicide. It had been one of my nighttime routines of years past in Harrisburg, and was now again.

-10-
(displacement)

In the morning, we were still without hot water, but the apartment was slightly less frigid.

"You can't do anything right. I drove that truck all the way here and now I can't even take a fucking shower."

We howled and cursed through a cold shower, standing naked together in the tub. Izabela moaned and insulted me, while I remained helpless to avoid or interrupt fevered thoughts of the misery of death factories like Dachau or Bergen-Belsen, and the showers camp prisoners were forced to take there. My helplessness made me wish that Izabela was an alcoholic too.

Sam wandered into the bathroom, and seeing him then, I didn't mind the cold water so much. Izabela saw him too, and immediately flicked a handful of water into his face. He bolted. I leaned into Izabela, close enough to feel her erect nipples against my right arm, and growled: "Don't ever do that again."

"Fuck you, and fuck that cat." "Just remember what I said."

"Fuck you."

There was a steely confidence in her voice, but she was flinching away from me.

"Go ahead, you stupid man. It would be the dumbest thing you've ever done."

I got out then, and found some clean clothes. I proposed that we walk to a nearby diner for breakfast. It was Sunday, and she had to return to Baltimore that same afternoon. I dressed quickly, then fed Sam. It was taking Izabela an eternity to finish in the bathroom, so I quickly assembled my stereo system from several old boxes, patched in the RCA cords and the speaker wire, and placed a CD in the tray. I could hear her singing in there, one of her own childish songs: "sheeeee was...a Perrrrrr-sian cat, a little *kiiiiii-tty* cat, and I loved her soooooooooooooo..."

I tried to block out the sound, but quickly thought better of playing music, for this would surely cause a fight. I'd made the mistake of telling her that I *liked* her music, which brought on a slew of pointed inquiries from her about the various subtexts of her rubbish lyrics, and a lot of singing such as her bathroom performance of that moment. I endured. I panicked. Then I endured some more.

We ate French toast with plastic forks on paper plates somewhere along that yuppie racetrack main drag at noon, and then she was one. For all my hatred, it struck me down to watch her drive away. I no longer knew how to be alone. I went upstairs, paced back and forth, looking out the windows, and smoking cigarettes. I took out the typewritten pages of my failed novel about Sarah, and taped the sheets to the largest wall of the front room, acing the windows. I taped them up in rows, in neat formations. I set up my computer desk and my computer, and a plastic utility table that would be used for meals, and type-writing on a small manual. I assembled cheap plastic shelving and finally played some music I wanted to hear. I held my cat, kissed him on the head, and considered calling Izabela. But five minutes later, I seized upon the first of my nights in Harrisburg's bars. I had fifty dollars in my pocket.

I set out on foot along Second street, scouting the neighborhood, learning my options. Across the street from my building were a three story gay disco, a hippie coffeehouse, and a beer and whiskey joint, also gay. I was painfully aware of my anonymity and invisibility, just as I'd been during my days at the YMCA. But then, at least I had the security of work, and the notion that in my 20s, a compromise of sorts would be reached, or at least a touch of good fortune would have to come my way. There had been several great purgings since then, several floods, and I felt that my time was up, and that nothing was left. I couldn't even cadge free drinks at the gay bars, no longer being passable as chicken-meat, or rough trade. My face was bloated with drink, my eyes drooped, my jaw was permanently clenched, and I reacted to any social advance like a spooked rabbit.

My attempts to mask this fear made my condition twice as obvious, and through the distrustful, prying eyes of a provincial, clan-sheltered nincompoop, himself like a spooked German shepherd, the sickness which festered within me would be amplified even further. I didn't want to be harboring this ache to perform violence on people, and their dogs, but it was growing in me. Betraying these feelings inadvertently caused me to feel as though I'd been caught masturbating in a men's room; I was ashamed of having rage and contempt, but when drunk, I'd become sympathetic, a synthetic sympathy that I gave myself over to, just as I'd give myself over to the inertia and idiocy of people readily the more I guzzled.

But always, always: I had the down-at-the-mouth, hangdog presence and appearance of a man who was not comfortable in his skin or in his present company. I felt sorry for the people I would find out there in the night, but I was lonely, and needed to confirm my civility, however disingenuous, and I resigned myself to the search regardless. If even one out of ten social performances came off as cordial or non-panicked or comprehensible, if I could convince only one person that there was goodness in my heart, that I was in truth a kind soul, perhaps I could start believing it myself.

As it was, the final whimpers of Hank reverberated throughout me, at times to the extent that his memory would ricochet from one part of my skull to another, a white-hot thing trapped between hard surfaces where it could find no release. In the corner of my vision, I saw the soft bulk of him hit the cement upon release from the dog's mouth, with one last muted shriek, after which he went immediately into shock, with a broken jaw. I couldn't let it go. I was so desperate to rid myself of it, so sleep deprived and guilt ridden that I guzzled hurriedly and when drunk, my temporarily reinstated enthusiasms made me appear barking mad. Perhaps it was apparent that I was flirting with the possibility of a random physical assault.

The streets were frozen, and the sky which that afternoon had spoken of snowfall was now making good on the threat. I sat on a riverside bench wondering what became of my wife in the prevailing years, to the extent that after warming up in several neighborhood taprooms, I made my way 2 miles uptown, swooped down an alley, past the supermarket where I'd worked, and surveyed the house where we'd lived together.

I stood there for fifteen minutes, trying to prize some distant memories out of the place, before realizing that it wasn't even the right house. I walked up and down the alley, looking at the backs of these dilapidated duplex homes. I stared at wire-screened porches, dog shit strewn yards, disused lawn mowers, broken windows, damp wooden staircases. Every house looked the same, and by the time I'd made a positive ID, my toes and fingers had gone completely numb. Furthermore, the exercise was starting to feel pointless and silly. For all I knew, she still lived there, with her screwy white trash parents. I didn't want to see them. And if she'd gotten fat, which she probably had, well...I didn't want to see that either.

I turned back, walking three miles south surrounded by arctic castles, brick and mortar mausoleums. It was confounding and enraging to me that anyone wanted to live in a place like this. Why couldn't they see it as I did? They were miserable cowards, fat and happy in this cowardice. And they were warm and soft. It occurred to me that no matter my circumstances, a constant factor would always be exposure: in the summer, I baked. In the winter, I froze. I didn't regret this, but with the alcohol, I was feeling sorry for myself, because it was too quiet and too cold. I'd done so much since I'd left Harrisburg, yet in this city, I was dead. I fantasized about murdering attractive female Young Professionals to keep warm. I told myself that I would kill as a coward, I would kill someone who as vulnerable, or defenseless, but I would kill.

I stopped at a gas station and bought a 50 cent razor blade. I dropped fifty cents into a payphone and left a message for Alex, a former girlfriend who'd taken an interest in Hank, during one of my black depressions when I could talk of nothing but suicide. She'd agreed to adopt the animal in the event of my death.

When I got to the riverbank, I descended a long flight of stairs, down to the drink. The stairs kept going, but I stopped when the filthy, frothy water began slapping my boots. There was a bridge to my left and a bridge to my right, each a hundred feet above, and may be a quarter mile off. The headlights of cars glanced off the black surface of the subzero waters. There was a dark mass by my feet; closer inspection revealed it to be a woman's purse. I threw it and the blade into the river and walked home. Sam was waiting for me there.

The cold new sheets and puffy blankets, coupled with the carpeted, low ceilinged room, created a funereal scene; I felt as if prone there, in state, staring at a burning blue TV monitor, petting the cat or adjusting the system volume but otherwise remaining motionless. Sam held a vigil on my chest, glowering at me.

On my first morning alone in the Harrisburg death chamber, I watched a Hollywood teen sex-comedy over the top of Sam's head, his fine cream-colored hair and the odd dust mote wafting through the sunlight.

Light entered the room through a curtainless window that gave me access to an unsecure wooden fire escape. Although I knew nothing of carpentry or lumber, I could see that this structure had been created from high quality material, pine perhaps, and was held in place by strong steel brackets which were not rusted. There was a metal banister, also quite new. But the building itself stood in deplorable shape, and regardless of its recent purchase and installation, the landing outside my window had succumbed to severe water damage; the center of the landing was like a tortured and exhausted rectum, rotted clean through in the middle, while the putrid area around the hole gave way with great flexibility, like so much wet cardboard.

Although I was only on the second floor, I assumed, first of all, that I would be using the window as an entry point, if not also an exit, because I'd already started getting hostile glances from the other tenants, but also because my landlord lived on the same block, in a million dollar brownstone, the only non-tenement house on North Street. My second assumption was that the "asshole" of that second floor fire escape landing would have to give way at some point, releasing me into the alley below. I said a faint prayer for my knees and ankles.

That withering solar piss haze, a sickly shaft of back alley downtown sunlight, burned lazily across the room and across my sheets, it burrowed into my blood like an X-ray, a Harrisburg death-ray, and it shone through Sam's orange-cream coat, allowing me to examine all of the millions of ultra-fine hairs in detail. This nauseated me.

Hank had been an American shorthair tabby, with intensely curious, intelligent eyes. His brown hair, with black stripes, did not appear in my food, and I didn't notice much on my clothing or bed sheets. He was gentle and unimposing, which made me all the more willing to talk to him or play with him for hours, to stare at him in small fits of adoration.

But Sam was a different beast altogether. Because of his temperament, I could not minimize the substantial air/food pollution caused by his unruly coat with daily brushing, not if I wanted to keep my scar count underneath a thousand. Sam shook you down like a crazed beggar for the attention he needed, in the moment, on the spot, exactly when this need arose in him. And if he found you in a non-accommodating mood or situation, he was not shy about expressing his displeasure and disappointment. Part of me admired this, but all principle aside, it was an extremely difficult thing to put up with, and I would find myself losing my temper, screaming at him, or even striking the infernal beast.

Sam's formidable head and paws made up most of his body, and when his demands for affection were rebuked with flustered curses, Sam would not scamper off as most small animals will, but lunge forward, hissing and swatting at any of your limbs he could reach. The rage which would sweep over his ragged countenance and half-mad eyes was heartbreaking, after the initial shock or annoyance, because you knew that his rage was uncontrollable, and that his fearsome mood swings, much like mine, were the product of human kind and not his own. You also knew instinctively that he was terrified, or hurt, more so than just plain old mean, and that he had spent most of his life enduring exposure. Of course, this would occur to me much later, after the hydrogen peroxide or rubbing alcohol had dried in the angry, deep trenches he would leave upon my skin.

Sam had a strange way of hopping into his intended victim when offended. He would lunge, deliver a few quick but passionate bites, then retreat. Being overweight and slight of lower body; he reminded me of a badger in this way, or a wolverine, especially with that waddle of his, but he had the smashed in face of a fruit bat, and one eye drooped noticeably. His face and unpleasant personality would grow on me in time, but with Hank still slinking around my brain, and crying out to me from that barren gravesite in Northern Maryland, I found myself allowing Sam to hold court upon my chest; even reaching for a bottle or the remote control gingerly, so as not to disturb him, but his gaze was irresistible, so we would lay there like that, sometimes for hours. I would attempt to understand my devotion to the animal, straining my neck to find a new angle of his face, one which I might find handsome, or endearing, or compelling. I could not. He was a homely old cat to be sure, but he had become necessary to me. I resisted obsessing upon the contradictory nature of my cat dependency, or the many other contradictions which had been emerging in recent months. Ultimately, I didn't care about the reasons, not for Sam, or me, or anything. My only hope was that if something catastrophic was going to occur, it occurred sooner than later.

That night, I entered Brickbat's, a German-themed sports bar. Brickbats was home to a despairing admixture of young law students, overweight skinheads, and black coke dealers. The law students would flash their pearly whites and play dart games, while the skinheads were fond of listening to generic punk music on the jukebox, and the dealers entertained several women each, seemingly unable to stop laughing. Beyond these three categories, there was only the occasional lone hopeful, a twenty-something bachelor who appeared half-brain dead. I'd talk to these weirdos just so the young women in attendance would not assume me to be one of them, because, unlike them, at least I could hold a conversation.

On entry, I was immediately crestfallen: no less than 8 big screen wall mounted panel TVs screamed sports games, and everyone there was in the process of gorging themselves on nachos. A glossy full color banner hung over the bar, and another in the window, screaming: "BUDWEISER PRESENTS SUPER DELUXE ENDLESS NACHOS NIGHT AT BRICKBATS! ALL U CAN EAT 4 $5.95 DURING FOOTBALL SEASON!"

On the plates around me were leaning, cascading precipices of ground corn with buckets of orange and white cheese. Baskets of hot sauce and small plastic containers of sour cream littered the tables and the bar. The Young Republicans, yuppies, and lawyers were sequestered in a front room by the windows, while the rest of the patronage accumulated towards the rear by the restrooms and at the bar in the middle. Each glassy-eyed reveler had secured his or her own Nacho Holocaust and for most, the proposition was taken anything but lightly. Some picked at their troughs dejectedly, while some engaged the food with a grim conviction that was altogether religious in nature. Among the crowd were those who abandoned their sodden happy hour allotments altogether in favor of moaning violently like rape victims at the televisions, apparently unhappy with the athletes' performances. When the game would go to commercial, the disgruntled sports enthusiast would drown his sorrows in his nacho pot, beginning with a liberal application of hot sauce, while muttering to the man next to him about *the game*. People here seemed fond of muttering to each other while staring at the televisions. The game held them enraptured. I wondered what kind of explosion it would take to move these men to take an interest in something, anything else.

On their faces you could sense extreme and authentic hurt, heartache, even. I saw that look once on the face of a man who found a DVD of his wife sucking another man's cock. You could tell by his posture, and the manner by which the familiar light left his eyes, like so many caged birds, that the old boy would never experience real joy again. His eyes would light up at a mention of certain writers, like Charles Willeford for example, or when you suggested going certain places, like Coney Island. But such radiance was gone now forever, and there was nothing anyone could do about it. Maybe all of these men had also seen DVDs of their women sucking other men's cocks, and now, all they had left was football.

But the truth was probably that they were simply cowardly and afraid; *provincial*. Their brains were just not suited to any stimulation beyond alcohol, sports, and threat of unemployment. Everyone there had money, and could do nothing with it but buy cars, and houses, and bottomless bowls of fried corn. (Except the coke dealers and their women. They weren't eating much, of course.)

I had two drinks and made my way to the Alva, where I had never experienced such misery. I went to the Alva, where I had 20 years history. I wanted to at least make sure it was still there.

The Alva sat a block back from Market Street. You entered it as a halfway respectable sort from a small one way street which no one remembers the name of. A cramped and seedy vestibule, unchanged and uncleaned in many decades, would open upon a pay counter where I would typically find Amir, the owner. Concrete posts, serving no discernible purpose, lined the narrow sidewalks of the cobblestone alleyways in this morbidly quiet sector of downtown. Other greasy spoons and taprooms, situated in the bellies of parking garages, or in alleys barely wide enough for normal cars, could be sought out, but the Alva, with its large vertical neon sign and warmly dressed windows, was hard to miss.

At one time, two blocks away, you could dine at The Spot, a 24 hour sandwich counter, a throwback to a 1940s/50s/60s dope market. The Spot had beer on tap and fare as truly repellant as its clientele (most of whom were missing at least one body part), but the Spot was closed now, finally, and the Alva had picked up the runoff.

The Alva was once owned by Jews, and kept up as a stopover for hungry travelers. Less than 20 paces to the north, through the taproom back entrance and across another bleak cobblestone alley, sat the Harrisburg train station, an impossibly ancient, chokingly atmospheric structure. The station's basement was utilized by Greyhound as its city depot. My entire teenage history, from 1988 until 1996, was rooted in that lower level waiting area. I de-boarded buses there coming home from Miami, and Buffalo, and Charleston, and countless other east coast towns, in all manner of horrid and unsightly conditions, dysfunctioned by female rejection and all night journeys, un-socialized and uncivilized in my youth. It felt like a lifetime of waiting, of buses, and arrogant young women, it felt like death and failure, being back there.

Cabs would line up along the circular station driveway, and if a Middle Eastern hack observed you approaching this procession from the taproom of the Alva, he would scrutinize you heavily. Unless you showed him sufficient tender, you could very well be refused service. Whereas, those who emerged from the Amtrak station were afforded a generous confidence. The driver wouldn't even strain to make eye contact. If you ever intend to rob or murder one of these men in the parked taxis, your safest bet is to approach from the station.

The Alva was a regular meeting spot for Jamie and I in early 1996, when we were separated and trying to repair our marriage through counseling. There was a lot of late night coffee and holding hands at the Alva then, and I remember how beautiful my wife appeared to me on those nights, and how hard it was for me to find sleep without her. I worked in warehouses, and on loading docks, for $5 an hour, and I ate peanut butter sandwiches, fixated on my broken marriage thinking that I had fallen through the cracks, that only shit-ass winos lived this lonely.

I didn't realize it then, but I was an exceptionally handsome young man, fully employed, and were it not for my basic shyness and inability to operate an automobile, I could have found a smarter and sexier girl than Jamie, who, being a Jehovah's Witness, was completely fucked in the head. Amir, years later, during one of my stopovers from Michigan or New York, would recall the young brunette, who I thought resembled Clara Bow.

"You work out your problem then?"

"We got divorced."

"Ah! So you get divorced! So what? Many other women for you, my friend. You are very young, you find NEW woman!"

Amir liked me far better before he found out I drank…which brings me to the taproom. I never saw anyone take steel or lead or even get punched at the Alva, although in all my visits (probably in the triple digits) I never left without hearing the threat leveled at least once, sometimes at me. Most of the patrons, of course, didn't appreciate a young white man in their presence. They drank one dollar 16 ounce Steel Reserve cans, or one dollar 12 ounce Extra Gold cans, or one dollar 10 ounce cans of Budweiser, and in the pre-ban days, the presence of cigarette smoke was so outrageously unbearable so as to be the thing of pure myth: to withstand this death cloud, you had to be both drunk and smoking yourself, or simply one of the walking dead. The bar's staff was the latter, and it was they who frightened me the most.

I smoked crack in the bus station bathroom with the black alcoholics of the Alva, and on return to the bar, past the cabs and overall that vile cobblestone, I would be scratching uncontrollably at an uncontrollable erection, nursing a righteous sex vibe, muttering through gritted teeth "oh Jesus I need a woman about now"...the blacks would try to coerce me upstairs to the fifty dollar a week flophouse where, they promised me, they had a young girl stashed away, a teenage runaway they'd put the heroin bite on; a strawberry.

I would instead retire to downtown's sole peepshow, an overheated lycanthrope with hunger pangs and phantom twitchings from an important thing long since vanished. But no true regret, let it be said. I always knew damn well: they didn't have no strawberry up there.

This all came back to me, photographically and psychosexually, as I eased into one of the low swivel chairs at the Alva's rear-restaurant bar. The bar had always been equipped with a stereo system, which the patrons would argue over. It gave them something to get wrapped up in, conversationally, besides women, and women is what they fought about. To claim that the new jukebox was too loud was to say that the place had "urban character": this device seemed like something the government may have used on David Koresh during the Waco siege, or against Middle Eastern insurgents in Iraq. The jukebox sent a squadron of ball bearings, like angry African hornets, flailing out of the smoky air straight into your core, the minute you entered. My first thought was that the bartender had died and the savage drunks had taken over and begun running things in a vengeful manner, as they had seen fit to do all along. But an elfin, rodentine man who may have been either 40 or 60 emerged to find me there wearing a dramatically pinched face of unbridled animal agony:

"why so loud?", was all I could bear to communicate under such punishment.

"It keep them CIVIL!", he said.

"WHAAAAT?"

"CIVIL! KEEPS THEM CIVIL! THE MUSIC!"

"OOOOH!", I said.

I ordered a Bud can, which I was elated to find still cost

only a buck. The Extra Gold was still there, and the Steel Reserve. Steel Reserve is made with the cheapest possible ingredients, and boasts of a sickeningly potent 11% alcohol. I always wound up with a broken nose when I drank that, but managed to have more fun, before the crash. A young man's trade-off, and I was no longer very young.

It was now three days, or maybe four, since I'd spoken to anyone, including Izabela. Without a phone, I had something of an excuse, but there was the old public library just a minute away, and my mother had planted that fifty on me ("this is from your father, don't spend it on alcohol."), so it was known among at least two of my constituents that I had money.

With the widespread "urban cleansing" of all public phones, it wasn't unusual for people like me to drop off the grid for a spell, but try telling that to middle class young girls like Izabela, or to a proud lower-middle class believer like my mother, who seemed to think that the ills of one's existence could be cured with foot powder and potpourri and holidays. I wilted at the thought of trying to communicate with either Izabela or my mother, so when the waxen-featured elf returned to me, I ordered Steel Reserve, and got promptly inebriated, drinking and smoking and talking trash about gullible, vulnerable, and unintelligent women until 2 A.M.

Back on the street, I chuckled warmly to myself, as if Harrisburg and morning and Izabela and my mother and the rest of it were not waiting for me. Halfway home, a dumpy Amazonian whore tried to proposition me as I passed the famed Pennsylvania capitol building (a poor man's re-creation of the D.C. landmark). The woman's size made it unlikely that she had a vagina, but I couldn't be sure, and in the dark there was no means of detecting the outline of an Adam's apple.

"Virgin ass tour," the creature said. "Round the world. Fuck your cock dry. Twenty bucks."

"Ten bucks," I said.

"Ten bucks won't even get you in my door, sheeeee-it."

I turned the corner, wondering if the creature had coke or dope. I made it to the alley behind my building, ascended the wooden fire escape, leaped over the soggy asshole in the

2nd floor landing, and crawled inside. Sam stared at me with huge eyes, disoriented and lonely. I fed him quickly and made my way back to the capitol, but by the time I got there, she was gone. The city was asleep now, even the scumbags. I sat down on the marble steps and tried to take it all in. The only sounds in the world then were an eerie clanking made by a steel pulley against a massive flagpole, and the fluid stuttering of the flag itself, whipping in the frozen wind.

I sat for a while longer, hoping to get rousted by a cop, but even the cops were hiding that night. Heading home a second time, I was startled by a barking dog, and it was then, I believe, that the birth of the idea was complete. It was almost 4 a.m. when I arrived at the all-night gas station, where I purchased 2 microwave cheeseburgers and a half gallon of anti-freeze. I found other clinking pulleys on other flagpoles, other places to sit and smoke and think about killing pit bulls.

I didn't see a single person; it was as if the city had died. In actuality, it had. A city is meant to have a true nightlife, but here, as in many other places, the homeless population had been driven to extinction, or locked up in prison by police, all of them pit bulls on two legs. It would have been just as quiet out there on a summer night. When I made it back to the 2nd floor asshole and broke into my chamber, I was frozen stiff and the sun was almost up.

-11-
(down in the valley)

"PAMELA" © INTERNET CALL RECORDER, transcript, 1.13.09

-So is this how it is with you? You just-

-What?

-Four days. My father got your family's phone numbers, and he says everyone's been looking for you, since Thursday. You can't just-

-Hold on a second, I'm fine! But listen... this is horrible: this guy, I think he's next door...Strange-u-bating Al. He strange-u-bates. Do you think that means "masturbating strangely"?

-WHAT THE FUCK ARE YOU TALKING ABOUT? ARE YOU RETARDED? ARE YOU DRUNK? WHERE HAVE YOU BEEN?

-I've been here. I couldn't get online, but I have this machine that fishes around in the air for a signal, and I couldn't get a signal, and-

-You ever heard of a payphone? Your mother told me that she gave you money! Should I go back to seeing Joe?

-Who's Joe?

-JOE! The guy I broke up with to be with you! He's got a BIG RED DICK, and he knows how to treat a-

-I thought you'd been seeing Mike, with the foot-long dick.

-I'm getting a promotion, and my license, and my dad's going to be proud of me. I'm not going to be with a LOSER, you LOSER!

-Well, I just got the signal, the, uh, network. It works, that's why I'm back online. There's a guy *very close to me* who uses the name "AL STRANGE-U-BATES OFTEN". This is an

all-gay neighborhood, it's always been. And this guy, who probably lives next door to me, is strange-u-bating. Isn't that awful?

-Fuck you, Gene! I'm DONE! I'm going back to JOE!

END CALL.

My first instinct was to redial Izabela's number. I was still half asleep. But I called my father instead. He had just retired, at the age of 92, and no longer knew what to do with himself all day. For the first time in his life, he was expressing feelings of uselessness. He was enormously depressed, and had become despondent. I got him on the second ring, and he offered to take me to lunch.

I called Izabela back, but she simply said, "We had to TRACK YOU DOWN to make sure you were alright, and I get you, finally, and you're babbling about jerking off? I'll tell my father what you said! There's something WRONG with you Gene!"

And then she hung up again. I scratched my head, which was throbbing, and tried to understand exactly how it could be that -if she was indeed concerned about me- she saw no cause for alarm in my having to share an Internet connection with a phantom "strange- u-bater." I felt an icy shock of aloneness just then, and also of violation. Al had to be some kind of sexual predator, a creep of Dahmer-esque proportions, and I've always felt that cockroaches ought to be exterminated with absolute prejudice.

I'd not seen my father, Jasper, since my return home, and thoughts of him overtook me. Having grown up during the depression, he'd found a personal sense of pride, and of purpose, only through work. And my father's work was hard manual labor. He had been a janitor for the city newspaper since the 90s, but in the previous fall, they'd forced him out. The paper was downsizing, along with virtually every other newspaper in the country, if not the world. The death of the newspaper industry was no great loss to me. I could have made a comfortable living with my words, writing for a newspaper, instead of the body wrecking car washes, dish rooms, and other meat grinders to which I'd always been forced to submit. But without a degree, I was un-hirable, according to the white collared, pink bellied conservatives who ran intellectually bankrupt newspapers like the

Harrisburg Patriot. Straight journalism, particularly in stultifying idiot-factories such as Harrisburg, depressed me. Every word screamed "hick", or "Nazi", and no matter how adverse the effects of a city like New York on me were, a big city paper could at least offer perspective, and culture, and language, and dissidence, no matter how condescending.

I'll never forget an article I'd read in the Harrisburg Patriot as a child, about the destruction of a Civil War landmark in Gettysburg, by real estate developers. An angry local resident who participated in Civil War reenactments was quoted:

"...to tear it down this way, well, it's just NIHILISTIC!"

I imagined the old Harrisburg coot grinning with mongoloid satisfaction as the exotic word left his lips. In this article, the reporter spent the next paragraph proudly plagiarizing Webster's definition of "nihilism", gleeful in his instructive tone like a senile old Rottweiler with a piece of week-old road kill in its maw. I pictured the two men, Central PA resident and Central PA reporter, as chromosomally-corrupted Appalachian cousins, shitting themselves with retard ecstasy as they fondled one another in an unashamedly celebratory fashion. I saw this redneck-incest scenario everywhere in Harrisburg; I heard its loathsome soundtrack of grunts and giggles in the every utterance of sickeningly complacent, mentally crippled locals. And ever since, I have rarely felt any guilt in wanting to stab anti-intellectual hogfuckers to death with a barbeque fork, particularly those from central Pennsylvania, because somehow, they are the dumbest of all.

But my father loved Harrisburg; in fact, during his 92 years, he'd only left the region a small handful of times. His entire history was in those streets, and this, for me, was Harrisburg's only fucking virtue: I could imagine the man I still knew next to nothing about, as a teenager, tossing cherry bombs at windows, roller skating along ledges, encountering supernatural forces under bridges, buying penny candy as a kid in 1927.The memories brought him life, patched him back into the world via the main feed cable of family. But the loss of his job really had devastated my father: it took him out of the city, away from his memories, and back to his suburban apartment where he was restless and lonely. Jasper's newfound unemployment was in fact the second Great Depression of his life.

A man raised in an era of basic common sense had no use for things like psychological diagnoses and their resultant psychotropic medications. Every new generation is lazier and more prone to that kind of infantilism which is born of arrogance and entitlement than the one before it, and being a solitary sort, infused with my father's stubborn Depression-era sensibilities since childhood, I not only understood his feelings, I actually embraced them as my own. It was yet another barrier between my peers and I, one which I was most proud of. People my age appear to me always as spoiled punks lost in gadgets and fads and meaningless catchphrases.

Not that this shared prejudice opened any floodgates of communication between my father and I: he saw me as a deviant, a class-A sicko, a demon. I disgusted and terrified my father, who clung to memories of me as a toddler as a means of coping with me in my late stage of degenerate self-abuse; but I could not bring myself to feel remorse for how I'd turned out. To be, that was like locking a man up for having stomach cancer, and besides, even if I *was* guilty of something, my own horrors were far too demanding for me to give a fuck about apologizing to anyone.

Parents never stop to consider that their offspring could be a Charles Manson or a William Burroughs or a Gary Gilmore or a Marquis de Sade. Why should they? In the end, such an aberration becomes his own problem, a lonesome monster who can only be abandoned, but the occurrence of such individuals is rare, and after all, there are places for those who will not fall into line with the herd. Based on the odds as represented by network sitcoms and talk shows, the risk barely merits   consideration:

"we are decent people, and our children will be decent also."

There does not exist a better reason than this to vilify one's progenitors. But the hate never lasts; you must always forgive them, no matter what they've done. And they're usually the only ones to pull you up after you've obliterated yourself.

In dad's apartment (an entirely brown, cavernous

bachelor's affair which seemed to be decomposing from obscure interstitial co-ordinates, slowly infecting all broad surfaces with toxic mundanity), the only displayed photos of me were as a child. Conversely, he placed current shots of my brother Mike in a prominent manner, as well as small portraits of Mike's many wallflower girlfriends. I loved my father most of all for his eccentricities, but his inability to see how similar we were, in our general weirdness, and what I saw as tragic, anti-social qualities, was to me just another Gregorits eccentricity. American family tradition, no matter how unfit for it he had always been, was what moved him above all else: this man looked for signs of conformity, of filial piety, and of social acceptability in those around him, because they reminded him of how good life could be, if one would just remember to respect his mother and God and the president, if one could only carry on among the petty chatter of other small people as an emotionally frozen, human forfeiture, via a series of asinine platitudes and fictions borne of a soft-headed denial.

At the core of him, even a thickheaded or fearful man knows that life isn't any good at all; he has seen his friends become pussy-whipped morons and seen his family turn their backs on each other. He has seen women and whiskey exactly for what they are. He has seen the Second World War and Vietnam and the Khmer Rouge and he has seen capitalist bureaucracies fail the working man time and time again; he has been refused medical assistance and he has lived for many years on canned food and tap water. He has been a selfish alcoholic or a gambling addict or a frequenter of whores. In that sterile, doom-stricken country club of the American middle class, he has always been content to be the pool boy or the caddy. But he tells himself that life is good. He tells himself that manliness means never letting anyone see you cry. He tells himself that some people are just funny in the head, and he shrugs his shoulders and sighs "it's a damn shame, but what're ya gonna do?" when the subject of a difficult family member is brought up. He believes that life is good, having questioned little since he was a much younger man, and maybe not even then.

The yawning chasm of a generation gap would do for an explanation; it was more than I could hope to receive from the man himself, I suppose, although I think he did try, in his way, to reach out to me. He certainly was willing to help me with money, no matter that he had almost none...but as I would learn later, he did this only at the behest of my mother.

I drifted around in these thoughts, which depressed me, so I was happy to break free from them when I heard a honk outside and fled down to the street (using the hallway this time, like a normal person) and hopped into my father's car. The car was a small Chevy, aqua-marine, or maybe teal, a color that hardly suited him; his paralyzing fear of foolish spending rather removed almost any discernible personal taste from him as a character. He had no aesthetic preferences, at least none that I knew about.

Jasper had always been a thin man, and remained so, save for a paunch from beer, and the body changes common to a man of his age. His health was excellent, and he'd retained the energy of a much younger man. Dressed in faded levis and a well-worn t-shirt, his age was both well-disguised and transcended.

I shook my father's hand as I climbed in: he was missing two fingers from an industrial accident many years before. In his late 70s, he sliced off a few of his palsied digits in a vertical saw during an attempt to purloin planks of lumber from the newspaper plant. (He had established a covert arrangement with the driver of the lunch wagon, who was eager to take the plants wood in exchange for free hot dogs. My father knew, like I know, that the greatest food in the world is FREE food.) In the hospital, Jasper rested until the bleeding stopped, perhaps 12 hours, and vacated his room without a single word to anyone. The next day, he returned to work, basking in the concern and astonishment of the young female secretaries, whom he serenaded with Rat Pack tunes every morning.

Watching my father drive around Harrisburg had always been amusing to me; I enjoyed pretending to have never heard certain stories before: his Hungarian immigrant parents, his childhood friends, the city. But on this day, with ghosts running around in me and the chorus of laughter which had become an ever-present addition to my conscious brain activity, little enthusiasm was salvageable, and my father, in his sadness, was quiet also.

"Where do you want to go?"

"Up to you, pop," I said.

"Hey!" he said, grinning at me, "you know I got these koo-pons, for MAC-Donald's, see if you can dig 'em outta that glove box for me."

His love of fast-food coupons, and coupons in general, was infectious: he'd turned me into a lifelong coupon clipper, and certainly, I knew how to take advantage of food bargains. I'd developed a hoarding instinct which kicked into high gear at the entrance of any supermarket, when I opened the full color store circular announcing half price chicken breast, or "buy one get one free" pounds of Land-O-Lakes butter. He'd also taught me to appreciate the superiority of a good name-brand over the generic counterpart.

I fished around in the glove box and found several wadded up sheets of glossy McDonald's ads, with tear-off coupons for free Big Macs and milkshakes.

McDonalds "food" appalled me, of course, but I was able to conjure a fraction of dad's enthusiasm.

"G'head. See if they got anything good in there." "Oh... yeah... yeah, dad, this is a great deal. There's a McDonald's just a few blocks up on Front Street, if-"

My father shot this down with a grimace, and a contemptuous swoosh of his bad hand.

"Come on, Justin..." -like the rest of my family, my father would address me only by my first name, which caused me indescribable nausea; I'd been using my middle name since my mid-teens, after classmates and teachers had left me so swollen with murderous hate that a re-christening became one of the many, many actions included in the gradual and bitterly inevitable process of disentangling myself permanently from the redneck morass-

"...you know I don't mess around with nothin over here. Nothin but boogs over here, heck with it all. I don't want some boog touching my food, I... you understand, dontcha Justin? We'll go across the river, it's... they got a nice CLEAN place, alright? That's okay, right?"

My father was an old-school bigot, and "Boog" was his word for blacks. I noticed that as he grew older, he became increasingly uninhibited about saying "nigger". He spit the word out deliberately and viciously in my presence. It rankled me something awful, but it wasn't the racism itself: there was plenty to hate about blacks, obviously, but when a man sprays anti-black bile around in some kind of empty gesture so weighted down in defeat and self-loathing, without ever having considered the reasons to share a hellish disgust for the white race also, he exposes himself a bit of a white Uncle Tom, clinging to the belief of inherent decency in a white society that doesn't respect him any more than the niggers do.

While generally courteous to black people, Dad took the change in urban American since his youth personally, and Harrisburg was now, of course, predominantly black. Driving through a ghetto, he'd mutter under his breath,

"No good scum-bums, dirty bastards. They're like wild animals out here. Wasn't like this when I was your age, tell you what."

Sometimes, his invective would develop into a small attack on me:

"All your life, your mother dressed you nice, she spent all kinds of money on you boys, and you were dressed GOOD, you were such a handsome little sucker. All of a sudden, you gotta look like trash, you... you GLORIFY all this, this... shit, out here. I just wish you'd start dressing nice, your mom and me both just want to see you do well..."

Beyond all of this, my father was a better father than most, but he didn't want to know me at all. I suspect that my mother had turned him against me while playing the victim, because she seemed to enjoy being pitied, and her violence against me as a kid bothered her as much now as it had bothered me back then. Or maybe not. Maybe no one really understands family, and sitting there in a plastic booth surveying a cold rural commercial zone, with tractor trailers roaring past in plumes of road salt, amid the fast-food hustle of white trash Christians and teenage mothers and fidgeting fat fucks aplenty, I didn't understand anything but this: I was a lousy excuse for a son, and I'd feel a hell of a lot better in a bar somewhere, talking to some boog or stumblebum. It was growing dark, and we drove back mostly in silence through the grey and frozen shit.

When I returned to my apartment, I sat down at the

computer, at my dead grandmother's wobbly old wooden table, and brought up a list of available area "WiFi" networks. At the top of the list was "AL STRANGE-U-BATES OFTEN."

I logged in alongside the ever-beflogged Al, and dialed Izabela. She was crying hysterically when she picked up, and began moaning that she couldn't understand what I was saying to her.

"Are you calling me from the Internet again? Why don't you just quit DRINKING for a week and buy yourself a CELL PHONE? Why can't you be NORMAL! Fuck this, I'm calling JOE!"

She hung up.

It was early evening, and I was sharing network space with Al. In that Harrisburg vacuum, in that world of onanistic strange-u-baters and anonymous nocturnal lonelyhearts, I caught glimpses of squalid couplings, down the street at the Y, in small apartments up and down the block, at the three-tier gay disco, and in the flophouse above the Alva. It was a quiet city, and even the strange-u-bating queers were too "responsible" for crystal meth, no suicidal passion, no toxic insanity, just dumb animal alcohol mania, pedestrian sex drive, and opportunistic seduction fantasies. In that airless black void, I imagined Al peeping on me, maybe from across the street. I lowered my blinds and went to the bedroom and took off my clothes. I stepped into the efficiency bathroom and brushed my teeth. The tub reminded me of Izabela's brief stay, when I filled it with pots of boiling water for her bath. The hot water was now turned on, and it would be so easy tonight to draw her a bath. Thinking of that hopeless night, most of my last 3 years seemed all of the sudden entirely unnecessary. My body then became weak, as if saddled with the cumulative weight of it all, the waste of it all.

Nothing could be helped now. It would all end soon, it had to. No more weight; no more waste. But I had hot water. It would be one less thing for her to insult me with when she returned.

I put my clothes back on and went out for a bottle of wine. I stepped gingerly along each city block, past the warm bars and cafes, over the ice. My boots were unsuited for the terrain, but I was breathing the city in deeply, all the while knowing that nothing good could come of any sort of immersion in Harrisburg's fetid aura; the smart move would have been to build a wall against it, as high as possible. But inching along in traction-less boots, I allowed the city to talk to me. The game was to out-wait the city's malevolence, to stare it down. I perceived it as a thing which had been created to destroy me, to either reverse my life-energy, or to dampen it so severely that I would collapse from a kind of psychic black mold. My constitution was remarkable, but it would not hold out forever.

The clerk at the liquor store, an obese black man, followed me around without pretense, and reminded me four different times that he was about to close the shop. When I told him that it was only a quarter till eight, I was sharply threatened with a refusal to sell, and ejection. The city's other two liquor stores had already closed, so I bit my tongue. By all evidence on display, this rude vermin was twice as fucked as me. I chose a magnum of the Frontera Malbec, a tasteless and thin-bodied Chilean bargain wine, which was overpriced by two dollars. I took the bottle to the Harrisburg museum at Third and Forster and popped it in a small cement alcove where a security guard had discovered my wife and I making out on a summer night the better part of two decades ago. Just then I saw a drug deal happen in front of a Subway sandwich shop, through the frosty branches of the museum shrubbery. I scampered across Third to score.

The man was heading towards the river on Forster when I caught up with him.

"Hey man," I said.

"Whatchoo want?"

"Crack."

"You poh-lice."

"No cop. Let me show you my arms."

"C'mon, man."

Through the snow, in the creamy light of a streetlamp, I got my coat undone and pulled up my sleeve.

"Damn. Whatchoo call dat?"

"I call it I'M NOT A COP."

"What?"

"I'm no cop."

"Man, FUCK off."

The dealer left me standing there like a schmuck. Small steps, slowly, slowly: I returned to the chamber, up the fire escape, across the asshole, and through the bedroom window. I turned on the radio, gave Sam a squeeze, and began making myself an elaborate dinner of Italian sausage and rigatoni with mozzarella, garlic, peas, and a red sauce with cream. While the sauce was heating, I pan-fried zucchini until lightly browned, then transferred it to the broiler. All I lacked was basil, but by the time the bottle was half gone, I'd forgotten about it. I cleared the table of unused writing paraphernalia, and laid out the dinner. I played old doo wop, nibbled arrogantly at the monstrous plate of pasta, and got drunk on the Malbec while paging through an old issue of GQ Magazine. Three hours passed like this: time went out the window and then it was very late. I looked outside, and saw no one in the bars or restaurants below.

At 2:30, my computer came to life with another incoming call: Izabela. She said, "maybe we should go to Costa Rica."

"Are you fucking nuts?"

"I'm not the one who looks like Freddy Krueger."

"Fuck you, cunt. I'm hanging up."

Of course, she immediately re-dialed with an apology. Then she hissed,

"If we go, you can't drink. I don't trust you with alcohol in your system."

"It doesn't matter. I don't have any money."

"Well, if you fuck up, my father will kill you. If you Hurt me, he'll kill you."

"I'm not going."

" You have to go. I already bought the tickets."

"No. No you fucking didn't, either."

"I fucking BOUGHT them, GENE."

"I don't believe you."

"That doesn't matter. Just check your e-mail in a few minutes. I bought them just now, while we were talking. I bought them online."

"That was really stupid of you, Iz. I can't pay you back."

"Did you report your income last year?"

"Yes."

"Did you file your taxes yet?"

"Yes."

"You should be getting your tax return check any day, then."

"I'm only getting a thousand back. I quit working, After Hank."

"I don't want to hear about Hank."

"Well, I need that money. For rent, and groceries."

"For booze."

I hung up. She called back. It went round and round like that. Finally, I muted the speakers on the computer and went to bed.

I ignored Izabela for a few days, and got a job as a dishwasher at Brickbats. My boss, Dom Paterra, was a fat, red-faced Dago with acromegaly. He owned racehorses and used the bar as a tax-write-off. Dom had an odor problem, and an anger problem; he was a bully and brought his dog, a pit bull, to Brickbats every day. He would chortle repulsively when the animal would sexually assault the pockmarked young waitresses. My porcine boss was frightened by me, and told me immediately that I wasn't going to last long. I began doing everything in my power to convince Dom that I was a dog lover. His distrust of me evaporated somewhat. I got his home address from an insurance form my third night: a large estate in Colonial Park.

By my fifth night, my hands were cut to ribbons, and the wounds were all screaming with infection. I left work early, and picked up a fifth of Crystal Palace vodka with a 20 I'd found in the break room. I was a block from my building, fantasizing about a peroxide bath for my raped digits when I heard my name called from behind. Of course, it was my spoiled Polish dingbat.

Izabela was fuming: she'd invested a lot of time and energy in finding ways to subtly advertise the fact that she'd been sleeping with other men back in Baltimore, and I'd been feigning obliviousness. Evidently, she could bear her burden no longer, and she confessed on the spot, right there at the front door of my building, during a heavy snow, beside a couple of discarded Christmas trees. I refused to show anger about it, although I was somewhat hurt. I felt nothing close to protective or possessive of Iz, but it was just a reminder of every relationship in which I *had* cared deeply, a reminder that I'd been gutted too many times, that people were mindless and Godless, that I was not safe with anyone.

We walked to the river instead of going upstairs. We were both secretly enjoying the drama of it; it was all we had left between each other. For me, it was all I had in the world, the only thing that made me feel as if I existed at all. Still, nothing was said, at the river, and nothing was said on the walk home. I was prepared to let her go.

On arrival back at my building, shivering and hungry, I invited her in. On the way up the stairs, she burst open with all of it at once:

"Everyone was right. You really are an asshole. You don't even have the balls to hit me."

"I'm sorry."

"I thought you were a man. But you're just pathetic."

"Why did you come here, if that's how you feel?" "You want me to go?"

I didn't say anything, but left her there on the staircase by herself. She followed behind me, and a mockery of a Hollywood movie hate-fuck scene transpired lazily. The minute I'd removed my prick from her ass, she began berating me again. I knew that if I struck her, I'd go to jail for at least a year, and be looking over my shoulder for another year or two after I got out. I also knew that sooner or later, she'd push someone too far, even one of her faggoty Nick Drake-with-autism boyfriends, but no matter how badly I or someone else bloodied that horrific gap-toothed grin, she'd never learn. In fact, the worse the pounding she received, the worse she would become. I promised myself that I'd take a bus to Baltimore with the sole intention of slashing her tires at the next opportune moment, and tried to satisfy myself with that. It didn't work. What I wanted was to strike her into silence, with a pair of brass knuckles, or a bicycle chain. I wanted her to shut the fuck up, once and for all, and I wanted to use a cruel instrument to do it. I wanted to prove to her how wrong she was: if I was only just man enough to put her in the hospital with broken ribs and broken teeth, then that was still more manliness than Izabela had given me credit for. The next day, we began packing for Costa Rica. I quit my job, and convinced my father to keep Sam company while I was gone.

It reeked of catastrophe. In Costa Rica, she reminded me, beer cost less than water. In Costa Rica, sex and cocaine were also cheap and plentiful. I was convinced that I'd lose my cool and kill Izabela. I realized that I had made considerable advancement since my depressive stupor of the previous summer: I was at least eating again. This was my chance to save my own neck, to continue healing, to steal something of myself back.

As Izabela laid beside me sleeping, silently passing gas due to a torn and over-dilated asshole, I looked around and felt that Harrisburg dampness, the dampness of the river; the Harrisburg impotence, the psychological and intellectual impotence of hypocritical, bigoted Harrisburg hicks. How could I find health here? In Costa Rica, maybe anything was possible, and if not, if it went the other way, well... I still had hope.

When Izabela began snoring, I experienced a fit of rage. I walked to the river, drank a half-pint, returned. I packed a bag and called for a cab to Colonial Park.

It was almost 4 A.M.

Book Three
THE COSTA RICA EIGHT MILE
&
Book Four
DETROIT IS MY SHOTGUN
...will be published in November 2012, by Monastrell Books, as
DOG DAYS VOLUME TWO.

Pre-orders are currently being accepted.
$20 US/Canada $30 world PayPal:OUTLAND6000@Gmail.com

The following is an excerpt from "Sex On the Beach", which will be
featured in *HATCHET JOB: The Gene Gregorits Reader*, published by
the author in the summer of 2012.

It is around midnight when she startles me from my reading: the most beautiful girl I have seen in several hours of wandering the boardwalk, and observing the strolling vacationers from breezy tavern patios. I am in an underground dive bar called Pepper's Tavern, considering the right time to have my historic return to the Atlantic depths. I've been here since around seven, and I've been writing fevered juicehead nonsense on napkins. I've been alternating between my juicehead nonsense and surface talk with strangers on either side of me, talking about *Exile on Main Street* and the Sex Pistols, about the tavern and about Ocean City. People are more sociable and more inebriated while on vacation. I'm no exception.

When I find myself alone ,I return to either scribbling or the disintegrating book, Norman Mailer's Pulitzer winner tale of Gary Gilmore's blues. The motel built above our heads is the Sea Scape, one of the cheapest boardwalk-side tourist dives in OC. I remember it well. My mother checked us into a room here on at least four or five occasions. We always seemed to get the same room, I think it was number 19, on the first floor. My mother would gripe about the squalid rooms, she would gripe about being poor. The Sea Scape was never too shabby for my father, and I much preferred it over the three and four star places, long before I knew what went on in the rooms. It wasn't the jaundiced old wino flavor of its economy digs that won me over, but the speediness of check-in and check-out, the narrow hallways, the lack of bellhops and serving trays. In a ritzy place like the Holiday Inn, there were a million things to get caught on between your room and the water. The Sea Scape always gave me the thought that it might as well have been built right in the drink. The Sea Scape was a joke to the other members of my family, but today, I love it more than ever.

Their logo is the same in two thousand seven.   The rooms are the same in two thousand seven.

The more that I think about it, nothing has changed at all... except us.

A lot can happen to a family over so much time... especially a family like mine.

Same logo.

Same rooms.

Same ocean.

In two thousand seven, I have checked in alone, to room number twenty six.

My bag is stashed in there, with my untouched swim shorts.

When I put them on, it will be different than before.

My legs were so pudgy as a kid. I had such fat little legs.

And my hair was more than blonde; in the sun it would go dead white.

***

The girl leans there to my left and stares at me. The barman comes over, she asks for a vodka cranberry. He asks for I.D. When she speaks, turning on the charm because she hasn't got I.D., I hear a soft girlish voice but with a very hard Russian accent.

"State law," the man says. "I'm sorry."

With that, he's off to the other end of the bar. But this Russian girl remains in place, and begins her stare once again.

"You can help me?"

"Me? Can I... no, I'm really sorry. I don't have any I.D. either."

"But they serve you drink? Why they do not ask for card?"

"I don't know."

"How old you are?"

"30. Nearly31 actually."

"Ah! You do not look theyr-tee!"

She grows silent. When I look backup, I expect her to be gone, but she isn't. Her short black hair contrasts harshly against her skin, which is as pale as mine. I'd guess her age somewhere between 16 and 22, but it's hard to tell in the bar lighting. Her complexion isn't the best, reinforcing my suspicion that she is underage, but a beautiful little thing all the same. She's wearing a raspberry colored mini-skirt and a Mexican-style jacket that only goes halfway to her hips.

"You have girlfriend?"

I nearly choked on my beer.

"No, do you have boyfriend?"

"I have friend who is a boy, but I do not have boyfriend."

Just then, the barman returned.

"I hate to interrupt man, but she can't stay here without I.D.

State law."

"Okay, I go."

The girl glared at the large, barrel-chested man and then gave me a similar look.

"What is your name?"

"Gene."

"I am Dolly. In room theyr-tee seeks, maybe you come?"

Before I could begin stammering, she was gone. Her purse smacked me on the shoulder on her split second exit-whirl.

"Not bad." The barkeep grinned, and shook his head. "Be careful with those Russian girls. She's probably got a boyfriend waiting for you up there with a stun gun, or a taser or some shit."

"You don't think I should go up there?"

"Fuck no. What ya want for a shot, s'on the house."

I chuckled at the thought of what had just happened. Of course, I had a hard on, and the booze had suddenly gone to my head. I did my shot, went back to my book, and tried to read. I couldn't. I even wrote the door number on my book, just in case.

Maybe she was a cop. Maybe she was a highly valuable asset in one of those international live organ smuggling rings. I'd stumble up there with a six pack of Budweiser and a hard on, only to wake up two days later hooked up to an IV in the back of an abandoned Chevy Summit with one or both kidneys removed. No pussy was worth the risk of that, not even this little Slavic siren. And the barkeep had warned me. It was indeed a disapproving expression he wore about ten minutes later, when I called him over to close out my tab and prepare me a take out six of Budweiser.

***

As I left the bar, I stopped to intentionally lose myself, for a moment, in the womblike warmth and magically full-bodied life-force of both my condition, and the wild black beyond out there, both deafening and hypnotic. The boardwalk was dead.

Room 36 wasn't hard to find, even though the hallway was dim then, going on 1 A.M. The roar and hiss of the ocean concealed my footsteps as I approached the second door on the left. I found it unlatched, and pushed it open immediately, before my common sense caught up with me and led me back down the three flights of stairs and to the safety of the bar. There, on a king-sized bed, before a large open balcony facing the ocean, laid a half dressed and unshaven young man watching television and smoking a cigarette.

The half nude slob looked up, and mumbled, " 'mon in."

"I'm sorry," came my response, half-shouted due to nerves. "I think I have the wrong room."

"She's in the bathroom."

I ventured further, stepping gingerly over to a circular, pressed wood card table directly in front of the bed, and sat down, removing a bottle from my brown paper sack.

"I'm Bob," said the thuggish Cossack swine. He had black hair buzzed down close to the scalp, and a significant beer paunch. Would he be the one to perform the surgery? No, I quickly decided. Too young, and evidently he had too little respect for personal hygiene to have any kind of medical know-how. More than likely, he was the muscle of this cloak and dagger outfit. I stepped over to the bed where he seemed to have been rendered temporarily immobile, and shook his hand.

"Gene," I told him, holding the mercenary stare of this Russian "Bob". I sat back down and drank my beer. I could feel the ocean wind on my forearms and tried to focus on the blowing curtains until I learned more of this nocturnal scene. In my own grotesque and deviant way, I think I was enjoying myself, if only because this thing, this "Ocean City home coming/ Russian sex-fiend-slash-organ thieves with names suspiciously like American sitcom characters" thing was simply too much to process normally. Then, there was also the twenty or so drinks I was by now radiant with.

I could very consciously sense a transformation taking place. The resort town around me was becoming an adult universe, or rather, becoming a part of the greater adult universe around it, the real world, with frightening speed. Perhaps I was hastening this with my movements, through boardwalk bars and now in this room, instead of the alternate modus operandi, a more traditional day, one in which I simply sat on the beach reading about Gary Gilmore in between vigorous dips in the ocean, perhaps a few pages knocked off in my reporter's notebook, a more civilized attempt to understand what I was doing here. Of course, that's an absurd notion. I'm not wired to behave so delicately. I don't know that I'm wired to really behave *at all*. I was throwing myself in harm's way, I believe, as a rite of passage.

If and when I woke up the next day, there would be no "Ocean City of the mind", no more nineteen eighty-three or nineteen eighty-six or nineteen seventy-nine memories. No place of dreams, no swooning over what might have been out here in my Ocean City of innocent ten year old romantic dreaming, of that Ocean City mystique which was over the years re-affirmed by the accidental melancholy of Madonna's "Cherish" video or the sandy, sun-baked, salt-water doom in the one for Chris Issack's "Wicked Game". Passing mentions of anything I could somehow tie down to Ocean City, transposed feelings, faces, ideas.... all that I had inherited as an unreasonably melancholic child and as a dangerously depressed young man would cease to have valid currency here, after tonight. All the things I had absorbed from the world around me, some of them far too deeply, could no longer be so effortlessly fused with the oceanside torpor... the first glance and the last glance, just another vacation... I never wanted to leave.

It was becoming clear now, at 1 a.m., waiting on a girl in a damp motel room, that a huge part of me never really had. It was time to cut the cord. The booze would help, and so would Bob and Dolly. In the morning, I would have brought these streets, these boardwalk fry stands, these rooms and these waves, all up to date with my new system. With my spunk, with my blood, or both.

"You ever have threesome?" Bob muttered, from his station.

"The three of us? Now?"

"Sure, why not? You want?"

"Well, I don't know. I've never done this before, what if I can't get hard?"

"When you see her, you will be hard."

The dirty bastard was smiling over there, I could feel it.

The bathroom door opened, and Dolly stepped out, barefoot in a silk see-through nightie. I stood up and placed my left hand down along her right thigh, the other behind her head, and kissed her deeply, with both terror and relief rolling across the surface of my tired and pickled 30 year old skin.

I offered them each a beer from the sack, and stepped out onto the balcony to smoke a cigarette, and think a while. There was nothing to fear in these rooms. Just night people. Nothing to fear down below...just a place where the land meets water.

And Bob was right. I'd never been readier.

***

Dolly sucked us and fucked us proper. But every once in a while, she'd stop and try to convince Bob and I to do something homo, like blow each other. Bob would narrow his eyes and turn to me, and say, "eh? You want?"

"No....I hope that's alright with you."

Bob would wrinkle his nose up and grin. "Yeh. Not me either." Neither Bob nor I had any interest in directing the "action" as it were. We simply followed Dolly's instructions. She was clever, and came up with scenarios in which I could quite potentially lose my balance and slip onto Bob's dick (which, I am pleased to report, was not as large as mine), or another in which Bob's dick would graze mine somehow, but we kept outsmarting her .Time and time again, Dolly's impish exhortations to begin cavorting in a homosexual manner were met only with grins from her otherwise agreeable and dutiful servicemen.

Mr. and Mrs. Filthy finally sent me off with their motel room's Gideon-placed bible, after a long bit of sermonizing about the

Christian faith. (Dolly: "You are a man who is full of hate. You must not to hate, but to love. You must find favor with man or God will never forgive you.")

When I returned to the bar, it was past closing time but they had forgotten to lock the door. My bartender was cleaning up. "Ah, come on in, what the hell. How'd it go?"

"I had to fuck her with some other fella."

"Ah…. that. Yeah, I've been there before."

"They were Christians."

"They…. they were what? Christians?"

"Yeah. They gave me this." I held up the bible.

"Je-ZUS Christ. There's some sick fucks in this world, I'll tell ya. I guess you need a drink. Go ahead and tell me more about it, and the whiskey's on the house until I'm ready to head out."

Four A.M. found me on the beach, with another carry-out six of Bud, staring up across the boardwalk courtyard of the Sea Scape Motel.

With 20/40 vision, and seeing triple besides, it was impossible to tell if the lone human shape standing on the balcony of the only lit up room on the fourth floor was Bob or Dolly, but I stood and stared back at the shape for some five or ten minutes. The shape never moved, nor did I. Based on what I could remember of that room's placement in the hall, it looked to be dead center.

Room thirty six.

Nobody on the road.

Nobody on the beach.

I removed every last stitch of clothing.

I stripped down quickly, fearing police.

I bent down and buried the six pack in the sand, lifting one out for myself as I finished.

I took it with me, into the great beyond: solid black.

And as I drifted out into all that infinite blackness, almost unbearably electrified from the whiskey and the smells and sounds, it became impossible to tell where the sea ended and the sky began, except to keep my head above, and, of course, my drink. This may have been one of H.P. Lovecraft's fever dreams, and there I was, floating around in it like evil incarnate, destined to vanish forever, into the deep, black sea. Yet still, somehow, I could not shake this fundamental trust in my own innocence, the gnawing reminder that I could carve one hell of a hideous path through this life but the worst crime of all would be no worse than stubborn adherence to a religion that wants me more than I want it.

Dreams of a childhood, of a childhood in:

This place.

My dreams are the most acute symptom of a virus that wants to make sure I suffer.

A strange peacefulness consumed me, and all other thought was voided.

The water was so very, very warm.

And so very, very cold.

Black on black.

I was getting too far from shore. My beer was just about drained.

A quarter mile offshore, I hurled the bottle out towards Spain, towards France, towards England, and swam back for another.

Like Cthulhu was lashing at my heels.